THE RUPTURED FIRMAMENT

THE RUPTURED FIRMAMENT

A LABYRINTH OF SOULS NOVEL

BY

STEPHEN T. VESSELS, PJF

ShadowSpinners Press

Cover art by Josephe Vandel.
Book design by Matthew Lowes.

ShadowSpinners Press
shadowspinnerspress.com

Typeset in
Minion Pro by Robert Slimbach
and IM FELL Double Pica by Igino Marini.
The Fell Types are digitally reproduced
by Igino Marini, www.iginomarini.com.

Learn more about
the Labyrinth of Souls game at
matthewlowes.com/games.

For my beloved uncle
Fr. Jack Vessels
who walked it like he talked it
and never dodged me
not once

Acknowledgements

It is a gift to a writer to work with publishers who both respect the author's vision and provide constructive counsel. I am grateful to Christina Lay, Matthew Lowes and Pamela Herber for conducting themselves as true supporters of the creative process. Thanks to my mentor John Reed for reading multiple drafts and providing ever-helpful insights and observations. Thanks also to the many superb writers I am privileged to know who took the time to read and comment: Chris Wozney, Alan M. Clark, Max Talley, Angela Borda, Rick Shaw, Nicholas Dietch, and Marianne Knight. Special appreciation to my sister, Annette Lagunes, for reading thoughtfully and keeping me honest about Beatrice's journey. Last but far from least, I bow with hands extended to friends and family who have gone above and beyond to provide support and encouragement: Monte Schulz, Lisa Howe, Chloe McFetters, Ian Wood, Thomas Vessels, Evan Vessels, Eugene Vessels, Sergio Thomas Lagunes, Diane Lagunes, Mark Aikele, Oja Fin, Christine Logsdon, Robin Burrows, Margaux Hession, Patricia Smith, and Theresa Pirozzi.

Author's Note

For me, *The Ruptured Firmament* is more a sequel than a prequel. Although events in this novel precede those in The Door of Tireless Pursuit, themes and concepts in The Ruptured Firmament develop from the earlier book. However arguable the terminology, The Ruptured Firmament is intended to be read *after* The Door of Tireless Pursuit, not before.

Editor's Preface

Dungeon Solitaire: Labyrinth of Souls is a fantasy game for tarot cards, written by Matthew Lowes and Illustrated by Josephe Vandel. In the game you defeat monsters, disarm traps, open doors, and explore mazes as you delve the depths of a dangerous dungeon. Along the way you collect treasure and magic items, gain skills, and gather companions.

Now ShadowSpinners Press is publishing this and other stand-alone novels inspired by the game. Each *Labyrinth of Souls* novel features a journey into a unique vision of the underworld.

The Labyrinth of Souls is more than an ancient ruin filled with monsters, trapped treasure, and the lost tombs of bygone kings. It is a manifestation of a mythic underworld, existing at a crossroads between people and cultures, between time and space, between the physical world and the deepest reaches of the psyche. It is a dark mirror held up to human experience, in which you may find your dreams … or your doom. Entrances to this realm can appear in any time period, in any location. There are innumerable reasons why a person may enter, but it is a place antagonistic to those who do, a place where monsters dwell, with obstacles and illusions to waylay adventurers, and whose very walls can be a force of corruption. It is a haunted place, ever at the edge of sanity.

THE RUPTURED
FIRMAMENT

CHAPTER ONE

Squad cars and emergency vehicles clotted up the street in front of the upper East Side apartment building. Not a scene common to the neighborhood, a block from Central Park. Detective William Braden got out of his car and scanned the cloudless sky above the towers. Another sweltering August in New York. Braden hated heat as he never hated cold; there was a blind itch at the heart of it, a festering havoc.

The Townsley Arms was a deceptively modest brick and limestone high-rise of early twentieth century construction. It boasted the old-school trappings of a haven for the wealthy: red carpet with brass treads and rods on the stairs, a burgundy canvas awning with a gold-trimmed crenellated valence over the entry. Unhappy residents clustered on the sidewalk, onlookers across the street. A sanctuary had been violated. The status the building enjoyed would not simplify investigating a homicide within its domain. Braden climbed the short flight of steps and entered a small lobby with polished, black granite walls and a high mirrored ceiling, product of some bright designer's irreverent remodel. More worried residents crowded around the reception desk and up in the elevator bay.

Depaglio broke off questioning a doorman in a Pershing hat and long red coat, came to Braden when he saw him. Braden lifted his chin in query.

"Looks like a home invasion. Four DB's, two adults, two minors. Mary and Davis Crenshaw and their kids. Cleaning lady found them."

"Crenshaw? Was he a dentist?"

"Yeah."

"Christ."

"You knew him?"

"He did my crowns. Get anything from him?" Braden tilted his head at the doorman.

"No unusual visitors. Couple of delivery men, but they went to different units and he accompanied them, in and out. Door to door in progress."

"Where am I going?"

"Top floor, 1702."

Braden climbed another short flight of steps to the elevator bay. Riding up, he dreaded what he was about to encounter. Crenshaw had been a warm-hearted lug, with the crap sense of humor for which dentists were notorious. Braden remembered the man's daughter, a little spark of sunshine bouncing around behind the reception desk, making even the hurting patients smile. What bastard son of a bitch kills a kid like that?

Two grim-faced uniforms stood post at the apartment entrance. Braden flashed his badge and they parted to let him pass. He took off his sweat-stained pork pie hat and shoved it in his jacket pocket as he crossed the threshold. A crime scene tech gave him gloves and slippers. Braden put them on.

The short hall ended at a spacious living room. Dining room to the right through a broad entry—Braden saw the parents, seated at the table.

"Kids in there, too?" he asked a tech who was scanning surfaces with a UV wand.

The man nodded without looking at Braden, kept his focus on the peacock wallpaper. He'd had the joy kicked out of his day.

Braden wasn't ready for the victims. He took in the furnishings and space of the apartment. Too rich for a dentist's income, even a well-established one on the upper East Side. Maybe the wife had money—something to look into. The painting over the floral-patterned sofa might have been a Monet.

He went down the hall to the left. The master bedroom was a study in sophisticated taste. Antique vanity by the west window, dressers in some dark, molded wood, another costly-looking painting over the neatly made bed.

His and hers walk-in closets. The husband had been more of a clothes horse than the wife.

The bathroom was like a private spa. Flat-screen TV above a sunken tub Paul Prudhomme could have basked in at his most corpulent. Two showers, two washbasins, a toilet and a bidet. Yeah, someone had money.

He returned to the hall. A door adjacent the master bedroom was locked. Braden called for a crime scene tech.

"Locksmith's on his way, Detective."

Braden touched the door. It felt cool, like painted metal. Safe room? He rapped a knuckle against it. Sounded wooden. Maybe just a room with a safe or something.

The children's rooms made the bile rise in his throat. Model airplanes and Star Wars spaceships hanging from the ceiling, baseball pennants and movie posters on the walls in the boy's room. Shelves full of books. Everything tidy—no mess. Evidence of the maid at work. Even the air smelled clean. The ceiling of the girl's room was painted with clouds and stars, fairies on the walls, dolls propped up on pillows on the bed. Braden flipped off the lights. The stars were luminescent. The beaming, happy child stung his memory again.

Braden cleared his throat and went to the dining room.

There was no indication they'd been bound or restrained in any way. Somehow, the killer had exerted control over them, induced them to do as he bid. It had been done without any evident disruption of the home or its furnishings. Everything in place, orderly, to all indications in the manner to which the family was accustomed. Braden still wasn't ready to look closely at the bodies, instead scrutinized knick-knacks, the situation of the kitchen, alert to any sign that something had been disturbed. Maybe there had been more than one perpetrator. One person with a gun, skilled and careful, could get his way. Feed the hope mercy was possible, that at least the children might be spared.

"Sign of forced entry?" he asked no one in particular.

"None we've found," Thompson, the lead crime scene investigator, said.

"We looking at one perp, you think, or a crew?"

"No way to be sure, yet. If I had to guess I'd say one."

Go with one then. Thompson was meticulous. She didn't make guesses lightly.

The worst thing was the black stuff, staining their chins and clothing where it leaked from their mouths. No, the expressions were worse, mouths seized in rictus of terror, eyes still fixed on escape, devoid of the emptiness of resignation, the final acceptance almost universally present upon the dead. Braden made himself look at the little girl.

His lips tightened. "Poison? What is this stuff?"

"Don't know yet," Thompson said. "Could be something that blackened their bile. I don't think so, though.

It's strange stuff. If you look closely, it doesn't reflect light. Non-reactive to UV as well. Some kind of eccentric compound, maybe. I don't think I've seen anything like it."

Braden puffed out a breath. "What do we have—point of entry?"

"The front door. They let him in, or the door was open."

Braden glanced around. "Scour every fucking inch. I want this motherfucker."

"Me too." Thompson rarely let her feelings surface.

A young tech swabbing Davis Crenshaw's lower lip dropped the swab and snapped bolt upright, frowning at his finger. "God damn," he said.

"What?" Thompson asked.

The tech had a dot of the black stuff on his glove. "I'm ..." He went rigid and dropped backwards like a falling plank.

"Henry?" Thompson went to him.

The tech's eyes rolled back in their sockets and he began to convulse.

Thompson stared at him a beat and whistled like a screaming kettle. "Everybody stop what you're doing and vacate the apartment immediately. Leave your equipment where it is and go."

"What's going on?" Braden asked.

"Drop your gloves and slippers as you exit. Avoid contact with anyone else and gather in front of the building. You too, Bill."

"Thompson, tell me what's going on."

"Look at him. He had a reaction to that stuff through his glove. We need Hazmat in here."

"What about your guy?"

"I'll stay with him. You go. I mean it, Bill. Right now."

Reluctantly, Braden headed for the exit. "I'll get Hazmat." He glanced back at Thompson, kneeling by her trembling team member, sucked his bared teeth and left.

He called Depaglio on his cell phone. "We got a situation. Unknown hazardous substance. We're evacuating. Clear a corridor from the elevator to the front door, and cordon off an area outside where we can wait for Hazmat. Push any onlookers back another hundred yards. No one exits adjacent buildings street side until we get clearance. Tell the doorman to call everyone in the building and tell them to stay put. See if he's got a list of residents with medical issues. And shut off internal air."

"Got it."

Braden put in a call with dispatch for Hazmat, rode the elevator down with the crime scene techs. As he departed the building he called Depaglio. "I shut off the elevator we came down in. No one uses it until Hazmat clears it."

Depaglio nodded at him from down the street.

Braden lit a cigarette, stepped to the taped perimeter and scanned the crowd retreating before the officers pressing them back. He spotted a guy that looked wrong. He was walking backwards in front of the uniforms, grinning up at the Townsley Arms with way too much amusement.

Braden called Depaglio.

"Yeah?"

"Jerry, there's a guy about twenty feet to your right. Black, short, muscular, brown leather jacket. I don't like him."

"I see him." Depaglio headed toward the grinner. Before he got to him the man melted into the crowd. "Where'd he go?"

"I can't see him." Braden squinted. "He's in there, Jerry. Get the son-of-a-bitch."

Depaglio pushed into the crowd and slipped from view as well.

CHAPTER TWO

Cramped and unrested from sleeping on a narrow cot, Braden was released from quarantine forty-eight hours later. Jerry was waiting for him in the CDC station's lobby with a change of shirt. The roar of a jet landing at JFK met them as they went outside.

"Where are we?" Braden asked him when they were in the car.

"Nowhere," Jerry said. "Homeland Security took over."

Braden grimaced. "Suspected terror attack."

"Whatever that stuff you called Hazmat in for was raised a lot of flags."

"Did they identify it?" Braden detected reticence in his partner's demeanor. "What?"

Jerry shifted in his seat. "There's a weird factor."

"No shit."

"More than you know. It disappeared."

"The samples went missing?"

"No, it disappeared. By the time Hazmat got up to the apartment, there wasn't a trace of it, not even in the evidence tubes."

Braden stared at Depaglio. "It evaporated?"

"I don't know. Once the feds came in the information stream shut down."

Braden watched traffic exiting the airport. "Where's Thompson?"

"At her office, I think."

"They let her out?"

"Yesterday."

"A day before me? She was up there the whole time." Jerry kept silent.

"Sons of bitches try to bench my ass," Braden muttered.

Jerry merged onto the 678 into the city. "They're not going to let you in, Bill."

"First they'll have to keep me out."

Braden strode briskly down the white-tiled corridor to the crime scene lab, the image of the young Crenshaw girl hot in his mind. Thompson was in her office, going over something on her computer, a half-eaten sandwich beside her. She looked up and favored Braden with a wry, commiserating grin.

"Not a social call, Eileen. What the *fuck?*"

Her eyebrows bounced in acknowledgment. "I don't know much, and what I know won't help you."

"Try me." He sat down in the metal frame chair by her desk.

She grimaced. "I don't know how to describe it."

"Depaglio says the stuff disappeared."

She nodded. "I was sitting there, with Henry. I didn't dare touch him, and I was scared."

"Anyone would be."

"I kept talking to him. He stopped convulsing and went still. I thought he was dead."

"How is he?"

"He's in a coma. That's all I know. They won't let anyone near him."

"Jesus."

"I tried to examine the black stuff on his finger visually, and then … it just wasn't there."

"Did it evaporate?"

"I don't know. It's like I blinked and it was gone. I looked up at the Crenshaws and watched the stuff on their chins sort of fade away. Ranks high on my list of strange."

"That's it? You didn't overhear anything the Hazmat guys said?"

She shook her head. "They hustled me out of there."

"Who did the autopsies?"

"I don't know. But there was a guy who came to see me in quarantine. Wanted to go over the photos we took."

"Did he give you anything?"

"Not really. It was more what he didn't say."

"Tell me."

"He wanted to know if I'd noticed any anomalous tissue degradations on the bodies."

"Had you?"

"No."

Braden sat back. "Conjectures?"

Thompson sighed. "Well, gauging from what happened to Henry, the stuff migrates through the body with extreme rapidity. Much faster than the flow of blood. Body tissue absorbs it very quickly—it communicates throughout the system across cellular boundaries. That might cause cellular disruption that wouldn't show up right away."

"What would it look like when it did show up?"

"Impossible to say without more information. It might just produce a discoloration, or if the effect was more extreme, it might cause the flesh and organs to lose integrity, maybe even liquify and melt from the bones. But Bill, among the poisonous substances I've seen that transmit by touch, that stuff is by far the deadliest."

❧

Braden sat across from his boss, keeping his expression static. McCleary, grey-haired and stout, chewed on a cigar he never lit, watching him.

"How long we known each other, Bill?"

"Awhile."

"Twenty years."

"Okay."

McCleary smirked. "I'm saying I know you. When you go Chinese on me you've made up your mind, and nothing I do short of taking your badge will matter a damn."

Braden shifted an increment. "Don't know what you're talking about, Chief."

McCleary bowed his head wearily, sighing. "In bold and underscored, the Crenshaw case is Feeb's and HS's. We're out. More to the point, you're out."

"We bring nothing to the table? What about inter-agency cooperation? This goes down on my turf and I've got no insights?"

"Do you?"

"Let me look at the file."

McCleary shook his head. "Not my call."

"Who kept me locked up an extra day?"

"I do not know."

Braden studied McCleary. He didn't know if he believed him. "No way that was a terror attack."

"Bill—"

"The guy was a fucking dentist, Tom."

"Depaglio told me you knew the family. That's tough."

"Save it. He wasn't my brother, she wasn't my wife. Five-year-old girl, Tom. Five years old and the son-of-a-bitch made her drink that evil shit. In our town, and we're going to let HS call the shots?"

"They played the National Security card. What am I going to do?"

Your job, Braden thought, but didn't say it. "You didn't have to deal us out."

"Look, I'm not supposed to be telling you this, but they might not be full of shit. That stuff, whatever it was, they've never come across anything like it. They're worried it might have been a test for something bigger."

"And we dumb yokels don't have the band width to suss what they don't savvy."

McCleary slapped his hands on his desk. "Enough. We're out, and you're back in rotation. Bitch all you want but do it outside of my office."

Braden went to his desk and opened the facial composite program on his computer. He could feel Depaglio watching him but kept his focus on the screen. A half-hour later he had a fair E-fit of the grinning man he'd seen in front of the Townsley Arms.

He printed it out and tossed it across to Depaglio. "That the guy?"

Depaglio frowned, studying the picture. His eyebrows went up. "The one you wanted me to grab?"

Braden nodded.

Depaglio looked more carefully. "Yeah. Yeah, I think that's close. I didn't see him as well as you did."

Braden stood up, reached across their desks and snatched back the E-fit.

"You gonna give that to the Feds?"

Braden folded the printout and stuck it in his inner jacket pocket.

"You're going to keep after this."

"Nothing on my desk, right? Fuck this place."

"I don't have a rubber."

"Going for a walk."

He left the station, walked to Park Avenue and turned left, unsure what he was doing. A couple of blocks down he bought a hot dog from a street vendor. By the time he'd eaten it he was done with uncertainty.

His cell phone rang. Depaglio. Braden sent the call to voice mail and turned the phone off. He walked over to Madison and headed south again. The streets were deep in shadow, the sky darkening. White vans and black sedans were parked in front of the Townsley Arms. Braden spotted the DARPA insignia on one of the vans. The block had been cordoned off. Guys in suits with their ears wired kept watch along the perimeter. A few curiosity seekers stood at the barrier. They would find it a meager source of amusement.

Braden noticed a man on the far corner. He was scrutinizing the scene in front of the Townsley Arms with peculiar intensity, hunched forward, peering.

Braden watched him until he was sure, then strolled casually across the street. He made it to about twenty feet from him before the man noticed. Their eyes locked and the man took off.

"Son of a bitch." Braden ran after him. "Hey!"

He chased him to the end of the block and left around the corner. At Park Avenue the fleer ran straight into traffic, making a cabbie slam on his breaks and several drivers honk at him. Braden dodged through cars after him. At the end of the next block the runner cut right. When Braden got to the corner he couldn't see him. He'd gone in someplace.

Braden slowed, advanced watchfully. Halfway down the block he came to an open garage entrance. About thirty feet inside a car elevator was in motion, the attendant out of his booth looking up at it, agitated.

Braden flashed his badge. "A guy run in here?"

"Yeah. Right past me and jumped on."

The elevator stopped.

"What floor is that?"

"Three."

"Where're the stairs?"

The attendant pointed at a metal door around the corner from his booth.

"Stay here."

Braden ran up to the third level. He drew his gun and stepped out cautiously. Rows of cars receded into shadows in both directions. He heard a shoe scuff to the right, loped that way a few steps, slowed.

"I'm police. Just wan'a talk."

A gun fired. Braden ducked between parked cars. He peeked around the fender of a silver Mercedes.

"You don't know what you're into," a voice called out.

"Explain it to me."

"You think I killed them just for kicks."

William cursed, fiddled with his cell phone, wanting to record what the son of a bitch was saying, remembered he'd turned it off. "I'm sure you had a good reason."

Laughter. "The little girl was *sweet*."

A figure dashed into view and ran toward the end of the building. Braden shoved the phone in his pocket and pursued him, sure he had him. The bastard had nowhere to run.

Deep in shadow, the figure disappeared, like steam from a mirror. Braden searched about, still running, not understanding what had happened. He crossed the spot where the man had vanished, and space and time folded around him.

Chapter Three

Sister Beatrice Cloutier climbed the cold, stone steps of the chapel. All around her in the cloister her sisters were asleep. It was after ten; the streetlights in Loc Gwenhael had switched off, and every window of the Breton village was dark. The granite-walled dormitories of the nine-hundred-year-old cloister were black, gabled shapes against a moonless sky dense with stars, the cobbled paths through the grounds immersed in darkness. Beatrice did not need light; she could have found her way blindfolded. She pulled open the heavy oak door of the chapel and went inside. Bright to her dilated eyes, a scattering of small votive candles burned right and left of the altar. She made her way forward, steadying herself on the pews as she went.

Beatrice was old school discalced, and had not even worn sandals, as many of her sisters did, since she had taken her vows. She had walked through life barefoot, as her sovereign Lord had, her flesh ever in immediate contact with the surface of His blessed world. She was long since inured to the cold, and the soles of her feet were hard and numb.

She was old. She no longer counted her years—eighty-some, at a guess. Her memory was failing, her frail figure bent and withered. The doorway of death was clear before her, the graveyard of dead she had known alive acreage at her back.

But she was not yet dead, and she had a question. A deep, inner, yawning question that gnawed at the fabric of her soul. She had been a reader her entire life. She had read fearlessly the science and philosophies of many who did not share her faith. She had examined and mulled over legion thoughts inconsistent with her own, and every time her faith had emerged victorious.

But she recognized, now, on the threshold of God's greatest mystery, an uncertainty underlying her faith that she had never truly answered. She would place her question at the feet of her blessed Lord and seek His guidance.

She had been reading Saint John of the Cross, and Thomas Merton's reflections on the great saint's ecstatic verses, and saw now, at the core of apophatic theology, the nature of the question that had elusively inhabited her being laid bare and clarified: knowledge of God acquired through unknowing. The question was so simple and obvious it pained her. If her faith were true, was it dependent upon belief? If she let go of belief, and all she held certain, laid her mind bare and open to the infinite, would she find the God she clung to awaiting her in those fathomless reaches? If she emptied herself of all certainties and convictions, and let her mind travel free of arguments and conclusions, what would she find in that emptiness?

So clear, so simple, so true, and so terrifying—with this goal in mind she approached the altar to commence a private, all-night vigil.

She knelt on the stone steps before the altar, steps worn with polished grooves by centuries of knees, and began to recite the rosary, the beads cycling through her fingers with such practiced art it required no thought, the words so oft repeated they had broken from meaning and become murmured sounds, a droning chant that conveyed her to a hypnagogic state, an inner twilight between wakefulness and sleep.

She was a professional. She knew how to inhabit this state with awareness. Awareness of the presence of God around her, enveloping her in His loving embrace. Always a comfort, but this night her purpose was not to reside in that awareness and surrender to its assurances, but to examine it.

She found herself, as was often the case, rapt in contemplation of the suffering visage of Christ, a vivified version of the one that occupied the corpus on the crucifix above the altar before her. His face changed, transcending its sacrificial submission to human cruelty and acquiring an aspect of supreme benevolence and benign power,

power that radiated from His beatific visage with the ameliorating quality of grace, so mighty that all wickedness and harm dispersed before it like dust taken by an explosive wind, not destroyed but restored to an unsullied purity, unified with the conquering grace in the way that love and forgiveness can translate the bonds of fear into an ecstasy of release.

Still, reflecting upon this familiar impression of Christ, her prayers reverberating through the systems of her physical self—her organs, bones, blood and being, even to the benumbed soles of her feet—she remained intent upon her purpose, held a little apart from the perceptual assumptions to which she was habituated, and posed the question, less by words than intent: what, of this, of all she experienced in her mind and senses, what, with certainty, did she know? Was she, in fact, perceiving the reality of God, or did what she perceived as true and concrete and unassailable originate from within her own unfathomable being as a result of belief?

Her attention turned to that which she had, through long practice, assigned to reflexive repetition: the words of the prayers she intoned. *Our Father, who art in Heaven ... Holy Mary, Mother of God ...* With these words, and the articles of faith, she had bound her mind and relinquished doubt. The rightness of this had been confirmed and reaffirmed by protean transcendence, freedom from ambition and want, the warm embrace of community, and compassion for humanity. None of which altered the fact of her decision to surrender to the will of a God she knew only by the implications of her senses, which had themselves responded to the same decision facilitated by the transport of words.

Words which she had not possessed upon her arrival to this world; words she had learned long after the reality of her birth.

Beatrice surrendered to her history, tracking back through the degraded pathways of her aging memory, through the shadow realms of revision, distillation and diminishment that constituted the residual story of her life—the story by which she defined her identity, the labyrinth of her journey with words. Beyond a certain limit, the journey backwards became intuitive, for she could remember nothing of who or what she had been before she acquired at least a fledgling facility with a language common to others. It had been with words that her history had become anchored: *I remember, I remember, I remember.* But before that, before she had known words, before she learned to identify a tree as a tree, a flower as a flower, a face as a person named, still she had possessed consciousness, still there had been meaning and thought and intelligence, still she had known and understood, and still there had been language, private language, known to none but herself, made of sights and smells and tastes and sensations and sounds and a turbulence of emotions that stormed above, beneath and throughout her earliest experiences of life.

And she had learned. She had learned, and she had learned, and she had learned, and she had learned, desperately, desperately, for it had been clear from the outset that the reality she inhabited was rife with dangers and uncertainties. She needed to learn, to communicate, to accommodate the monstrous others who surrounded her, the gods she came to know as Mother and Father, upon whom she relied for survival.

That private, self-referenced language Beatrice saw was still alive within her, the language of her senses, from which every word she had ever spoken was in fact a translation, and via which every word she had ever read or heard was interpreted. But what had she known, what had she believed, before she had learned the word, "Believe?"

The face of her sovereign Lord, radiant with the gentle power of infinite forgiveness, wavered in her mind, and she had a vision that she could not with surety ascribe to fantasy or remembrance. She saw the bars of a crib about her, and beyond a window. On the sill of the window stood a potted plant: a tulip in full bloom, basking in the light of an unseen sun.

Beatrice, still intoning the prayers of the rosary, unaware, now, of doing so, the words having become vibrations, wept and did not know why. She experienced a profound taste of salt in her mouth and knew in a direct and physical way that she could never have explained that this *was* memory, *true* memory, from a time before she had known what memories were. How many times, attending baptisms, had she watched the priest place blessed salt in the mouth of a newborn?

She experienced a translation of her being, a transubstantiation of all that she knew as physical and real into a condition beyond what she knew or understood to be known. She departed the realms of knowledge, and entered a state of pure being, unburdened by thought. And in that state, she ceased to pray and inhabited a continent of silence.

Some unknowable measure of time later she blinked and opened her eyes and found herself lying prostrate on the floor of a vast cavern with luminous walls.

Chapter Four

William Braden stared in comprehensive bewilderment at tall buildings, an immense thoroughfare bustling with traffic, throngs of jostling pedestrians, unable to process that the city extending about him was most certainly *not* New York. Giant LED displays on the surrounding towers conveyed messages neither in English nor the English alphabet. The people on the broad sidewalk all seemed to be Asian. They avoided eye-contact, though many frowned, walking around him. He was an impediment in the flow, an island of confusion in a sea of people who knew where they were and where they were going.

One person did return his gaze. A white-haired man watched him from a short distance away. The old man approached and said something in what might have been Japanese. Nothing going on in Braden's head could have formulated a response.

The old man's frown deepened. "You should not quicken into public like this," he said.

The words were English but made no sense. "I'm …" A consuming sensation Braden did not understand and could not control babbled through his body. "Where am I?"

His legs buckled. The old man caught him and guided Braden to the boulevard's edge. "What's going on?"

The old man didn't answer. A cab pulled up. The old man pulled open a door. The world shifted to the right and back repetitively, like the whole thing rode a giant, stuttering cog. The edges of vision dimmed. Braden slumped into the back seat of the cab and passed out.

⤙

He opened his eyes upon a white ceiling. He didn't know where he was or what had happened. Maybe he'd had a dream.

The room was in no way familiar. To his right hung an inkbrush scroll of a frog on a log amid an implication of river and a moon, long columns of Asian characters descending its left perimeter; to the left extended a paper screen mullioned with black strips of wood.

Braden sat up. He was on a narrow bed. His jacket, neatly folded, rested on a cabinet of drawers, his hat on top. The air smelled pleasant and clean, with a faint, earthy scent. Braden remembered chasing the grinning man through the garage. Something had happened—there was a piece missing. And then he'd seen the man become shadow-like, running down a crowded sidewalk, and vanish like he'd erased himself.

The sidewalk hadn't been in New York.

Braden threw his legs over the edge of the bed, coming alert, fully awake. Memory of how he'd traveled from one city to another was a void. He must have been knocked out or something. Drugged. But that didn't feel true.

Something serious had happened to him. Maybe he'd had a stroke. His uncle had had one in his forties. How much time had he lost? Days? Weeks? Fear seized him like a phantom serpent. *Years?*

His shoes had been removed. By the bed was a pair of slippers. Braden pulled them on. *Focus on the next thing. In the absence of understanding, seek answers. Evidence. What is known, what is knowable. Narrow the question, divide it into manageable parts.* The first thing he needed to know was where he was.

Light filtered through a window concealed by paper shutters. Braden stood and opened the shutters. A view of an apartment building, the width of a narrow street distant, confronted him. Balconies neatly lined with potted plants, here and there clothes on drying racks. Neither the top nor the base of the building was visible through the window.

Faint sounds issued from beyond the paper screen. Braden found a groove in the right edge and slid the screen open. He was in a small apartment. A long, low wooden table, with cushions on either side, centered the room before him. The left wall was lined with shelves of books, a sliding glass door at the near end. Through the latter was a small balcony where several miniature, potted trees rested on a wooden bench. A desk faced the wall opposite the books. Past that was a cramped kitchen.

A white-haired man stood over the stove, preparing something in a clay pot. He looked up at Braden. "Gaiji," the old man called out.

A young man with neatly trimmed black hair emerged from a room down a short hall to the right. He bowed to Braden. By instinct Braden bowed back.

The young man opened his hand at the long table, continuing to bow, and motioned for Braden to sit down. Mystified, Braden sat.

"Where am I?" he asked the young man.

"My uncle will explain," the young man answered. "Do not be distressed, please. You are safe, here."

The old man said something in Japanese, and the young man withdrew. The old man poured liquid out of the clay pot. He emerged from the kitchen bearing a small bowl in his hands. Bowing, he offered the bowl to Braden.

"Drink this," the old man said. "It is good for your *ki*."

"My what?" Braden accepted the bowl uncertainly, bowing again as he did so.

"Your life force. You have had a most severe shock."

Braden frowned at the dark fluid in the bowl, smelled it. It was the source of the earthy scent in the room. "What is it?"

"A tea of some medicinal herbs. You may find the taste a bit strange, but it will help you."

Braden decided to play along. It seemed unlikely that the old man would have brought him to his home and given him a place to sleep if he'd wanted to poison him. He sipped the tea. The flavor did not recommend it. Something like how a warm mud puddle might taste. But it felt good going down. Braden felt a little steadier—calmer in the face of the incomprehensible. He took another sip, more to be polite than comply, and set the bowl on the table.

"Thank you."

The old man sat down beside him. "Permit me to introduce myself, Detective Braden-san. I am Tanizaki Yoshiro. Please call me Yoshi."

Braden sniffed a couple of times and rubbed his mouth. "Let's start again."

"As you wish."

"How do you know me?"

"I took the liberty of looking in your jacket and found your badge and identification."

"You don't know me from before … on the street?"

Yoshi shook his head.

"Well, I um …" Braden cleared his throat. "I guess my next question is why are you helping me?"

"Because you are Quick, as am I."

The answer was nonsensical. "Quick? Quick how?"

The old man studied Braden for a moment. "It may be easier to explain if you tell me what you remember."

"I don't remember shit. I don't even know where I am."

"You are in Tokyo."

"*Tokyo?* What the hell am I doing in Tokyo? How did I get here?"

"You do not know?"

"I wouldn't ask if I did!"

Yoshiro gave Braden a moment to collect himself. "Again, if you would tell me the last thing you remember before we met, it might help clarify matters."

"I don't remember coming to fucking Tokyo!"

"Before that."

Braden sighed and tried to remember. There was nothing. He shook his head.

"Please, Detective Braden-san."

"It's not going to help. It doesn't have anything to do with me being here. Something's wrong with me. I've got amnesia. I've had a stroke or something. I should go to a hospital."

"If you wish me to take you to a hospital, I will do so. But first, tell me, please, what you remember."

"I was chasing a bad guy. In New fucking York, which is where I *live*."

"I see. And when were you chasing this man? What was the date?"

"August seventeenth. 2015."

Yoshiro pulled a cell phone from his robe. He turned it on, fiddled with it a moment, and turned it for Braden to see. The date was August seventeenth.

Braden stared at the phone. "What is that, some kind of joke?"

"No joke, Detective Braden-san."

Braden grimaced. "Wha'd I do, beam here? Fuck you. You're playing with my head."

"You quickened."

"What the hell does that mean?"

"You exercised an ability few people possess. You were in New York, and then you were here."

Braden started to object again, but thought of the thing he'd remembered upon waking, the man he'd chased vanishing into thin air on a crowded street. The street where Yoshiro had come to his aid. And that was the second time he'd vanished. Braden stared at the table. "He disappeared."

"Who?"

Yoshiro's expression betrayed no hint of subterfuge. "The man I was chasing," Braden said. "He disappeared. I was running after him, and then he was gone. I kept running. I thought he'd … I don't know what I thought."

Yoshiro's expression changed. "I understand now."

"Understand what?"

"Drink some tea."

"I don't want any more fucking tea." Terrible feelings, slithering dreads, grew in Braden. He couldn't escape them. The world had gone crazy. He'd gone crazy. All the human garbage he'd slogged through, the filth most people never saw firsthand, had finally eaten through his sanity. He'd known schizophrenics, drug addicts driven mad by cravings and mindless, willful self-destruction. He didn't want to live like that.

"Detective Braden-san." Yoshiro placed his hand gently on Braden's forearm. "Calm yourself."

The human warmth in that simple gesture reached Braden. The panic threatening to overwhelm him still lived, writhing and gnawing at his racing heart, but he steadied some. He held Yoshiro's hand like a drowning man desperate to climb in the boat.

Something opened in William, something old and forgotten, so old he couldn't remember when he'd last known it, maybe as a child, that the world was more than it seemed, and that beneath every doubt and cause for cynicism was something wondrous.

And within that, that *he* was more, that the self he understood himself to be was a product of constriction, of disabled imagination, of a series of decisions and conclusions he had adopted about life to spare himself the wearying task of defending hope.

Catch this person, that one, intervene where possible to prevent life from sinking to its lousiest potential; work 'til you were too shot to stay awake, go home absent wife or children and think as little as you could. Think least of all about the boy you once were, the stained and sullied dreams you once harbored.

Braden pulled his hand away from Yoshiro's comradely grasp and looked at it. He couldn't remember the last time he had looked at his own flesh with appreciation for its substance, let alone the marvel of its existence. And something deeper: the mystery of the self, a kind of song made flesh, chords that could echo and fly.

He remembered. The man, running away, then not just disappearing—with a different kind of vision William had never used wittingly, and not at all in so long that the faculty had withered, he has *seen* …

He hunched over the table, trembling, awash in emotions he could never have named.

"Gently," Yoshiro said.

"I, uh …" William cleared his throat. "You have any whiskey?"

Yoshiro produced a bottle and two more miniature bowls. William eyed the Japanese script on the bottle with skepticism, but a sip vanquished doubt.

"It is acceptable?"

William cleared his throat again. "Uh, yeah." He lifted his bowl in toast, and they sat awhile without speaking.

Halfway through Yoshiro's second pour, William said, "I need help understanding this."

"It is very rare," Yoshiro said quietly, "that one as old as you opens to the ability we share. Those of us who possess the ability, which we suspect everyone possesses, though most without awareness, call ourselves the Quick, and the practice *quickening*. You probably never would have awakened to the ability had you not pursued one who had. It seems you stumbled into awareness through your determination to apprehend him."

"How can a bastard like that—and I mean there aren't words to describe this son-of-a-bitch—know this, have this ability, and do what he did?"

"Neither understanding nor ability provide assurance of goodness. There is enough pain in the universe to turn a holy man cynical."

"Don't give me that. I've spent my life wading through sewage, and it's turned me just about as cynical as they come. I don't go around doing … *that*."

"What did he do, this bad man?"

"You don't want to know."

"I do."

William looked around at the small, tidy apartment, all the books neatly ordered on the shelves, the warm atmosphere of an old way of living recreated in a big-city high-rise. He didn't want to put the things he'd seen in this kind man's mind. "What do you do, Yoshi?"

"I teach English."

William grunted. "Are there a lot of … us? People who can do this quickening thing?"

"Very few who travel in this world. Fewer still who live here."

"I'm not sure I want you to explain that." Braden sipped his whiskey. "Seems like kind of a big coincidence, you showing up when you did."

"I do not believe it was a coincidence. I rarely visit that part of the city. For some reason, today I felt drawn to. You are evading my question."

Braden chewed his lips. "I don't know what good it will do."

"Nevertheless."

William sighed and described what had happened, being sparse with the details.

Yoshiro was silent a moment. "In your jacket I found a composite picture of a man's face. Is he the one you seek?"

Braden nodded.

"A man of dark skin, short and quite muscular, yes?"

Braden looked at Yoshiro and nodded.

"I believe he is known to me. If he is the person I am thinking of, he is very dangerous."

"I'm considered dangerous myself, in some circles."

"I do not doubt it. I do not know the man's birth name. He is now commonly known as Slick."

"Slick." The word tasted wet and rotten in Braden's mouth. "That's a good name for an asshole. Do you know where he is?"

"I do not. I may know someone who does. I will ask. Right now, there is more you need to learn."

William's attention drifted to the trees on the balcony.

"Do you know bonsai?" Yoshiro asked.

"I've heard the word. That what those are?"

"Yes. They are my teachers."

William grunted softly. "Looks like a lot of work."

"The reward is greater than the labor."

Yoshiro spoke, then, about the veil between this world and another that underlay consciousness and all human reality. Braden sat quietly and listened. He didn't understand most of it. Partly, awakened or not, he did not want to. It challenged too many assumptions he had made about life, and they weren't easy to relinquish. But he listened, until the day and the whisky took their toll and he grew drowsy. Yoshiro helped him back to bed.

❧

When he awakened next it was dark. For a moment he was disoriented, then he remembered where he was. His doubts returned to him. He accepted that he was in Tokyo, but the rest of it—he didn't feel sure of anything. Maybe he'd been drugged. Various unlikely scenarios tried themselves out in his mind.

The screen slid open. A dim figure stood in the entry.

"You are awake, Braden-san?" Yoshiro asked softly.

"Yeah."

"I as well. Do you feel rested enough for a small journey?"

William sat up and rubbed his knees. "Sure, why not."

Yoshiro turned on a lamp in the outer room. Braden pulled on his jacket and his hat. He felt his pockets. His badge, keys and wallet were there. His gun and holster were missing.

"You will not need your weapon," Yoshiro said. "I fear you may have to abandon it. It will be difficult enough to acquire you passage back to America without it. You do not have a passport."

"I thought I can just click my heels together."

"You do not yet possess the skill. But it is possible I know someone who can help."

"That who we're going to see?"

"Yes."

William accompanied Yoshiro out of the building. The streets were alive with activity. Braden started to turn on his phone to check the time but thought better of it. If Depaglio or McCleary called it would show on the records that he had been out of the country. "What time is it?"

"About three in the morning. Like New York, Tokyo never sleeps."

They boarded a train and traveled to another part of the city, where the buildings were older, shorter, and farther apart. They exited in an area dominated by private homes that were walled off from the streets. Here the streets were quiet.

"What do you want, Braden-san?" Yoshiro asked, as they walked up a steep avenue.

Braden lit a cigarette. "Call me Bill."

"Thank you. What do you want, Bill?"

"I want to catch the bastard who killed those kids."

"The things you described, how that family was murdered, may relate to matters beyond your capacities. The black substance you described—I suspect the killings were a kind of magical experiment."

"Magical?" Braden blew smoke.

"In the darkest sense. Although magic is a poor word for characterizing such practices. I only tell you this because I do not think you will find him in the world with which you are familiar. I think you will have to enter the Labyrinth of Souls to find him. I do not mean to discourage you. Only, you have no experience there."

"This the place you were talking about, that's behind—" Braden gestured at their surroundings.

"Invisible to this reality, yes."

Braden took a long drag and exhaled, wondering where he would wind up. "How do I get there?"

"There are many ways. The first crossing is different for everyone. I cannot tell you what yours will be. It will be personal, affected in large measure by your intentions. It will be a process of discovery."

They turned a corner. At the end of the street ahead stood a large and old-looking temple. The temperature dropped precipitously, and it began to snow. The walls lining the street vanished, along with several of the homes. Those that remained changed in character, becoming simpler, and somehow more evocative of a culture.

Braden stopped and looked back. The city behind them was greatly diminished, no longer the gleaming sea of lights it had been. It stopped snowing, the lane now unaccountably deep with snow.

"What just happened?"

"We have come where we need to be," Yoshiro said. He extended his hand forward and they continued toward the temple. Braden accompanied Yoshiro mechanically, too baffled to speak. He flicked the coal off his cigarette and put the butt in his back pocket before they climbed the steps. Yoshiro pulled open a tall wooden door and they went in. The interior was illuminated dimly by oil lamps hanging from wooden pillars to either side of a broad hall, where a few bald-headed monks sat on mats, meditating. At the far end of the hall one monk sat facing the others.

Yoshiro escorted William to a place near the front. He sat down cross-legged on a mat and motioned for William to do likewise. William's joints were not limber enough to accommodate the pose Yoshiro assumed, but he came as close as he could.

Yoshiro smiled at William, faced forward and closed his eyes. William understood he was to copy him.

William sighed and closed his eyes. Worries and uncertainties tangled through his mind. He could not master them.

He needed to understand something. He needed the answer to a question beyond his capacity to frame. This had always been the case, he realized. All the investigating he'd done, chasing after criminals—that wasn't part of the question.

School had bored him. He had never been a good student. His methods of learning had always been random and disorganized—bits of things latching onto each other until they connected in ways that made sense. A blood pattern, a phone record, a look in an old drunk's eyes. The shadow of a tree in a park, a song, a teacher he hadn't appreciated. He knew lots of things—he'd learned lots of things. But his knowledge wasn't organized around an objective or even competency with his profession. It was gathered around some deeper motive he'd never really examined.

A painful memory from his childhood awakened with clarity. He hadn't walked his dog, one day, as he was supposed to. He came home to find his father giving the dog away to a friend of his, a fellow cop. William's objections were ignored; his father's friend took the dog to his squad car. William remembered the dog looking back at him through the rear window, frightened and confused, as the car drove away.

Injustice, cruelty—what was that? What was its source? It was rooted in everything. Fear, confusion, frustration, the fucking mystery of existence—but that wasn't the question.

William opened his eyes. The monk who had been at the front of the temple was sitting immediately before him, their knees nearly touching. Without understanding the impulse, William opened his right hand. The monk leaned forward and placed a coin in William's palm, then closed William's fingers over it. The monk resumed his meditative posture and closed his eyes.

Holding the coin, William closed his eyes again, too. His thoughts and memories rambled on, increasingly dominated by events of his childhood. His mother sitting on the edge of his bed, reading to him when he was sick. He saw her face with a clarity he had not been able to summon in years. She sifted apart like sand, leaving emptiness. Both the question and the answer were there, in the void.

The air changed, and with it the texture of the place around him. He heard familiar sounds. Street noise, the hum of a city, rose in his hearing to a customary volume.

William opened his eyes. He was in the garage where he had chased the man known as Slick, back in New York.

Chapter Five

Braden stood up quickly, alert and watchful. He couldn't help wondering if he'd imagined the whole trip to Japan. His years on the force had been a body-building course for his skepticism. Someone could have knocked him out, and everything he 'remembered' be the result of time dilation in an unconscious state.

He didn't entertain the notion with much seriousness. His memories of Yoshi, the apartment, the train ride through Tokyo, the snowy avenue and the temple, were too solid, full-formed, and specific, even if they did include shifts in geography and possibly even time as preposterous as those in dreams.

He pulled out his cell phone and turned it on, waited for it to boot up. August twenty-third. He stared at the small screen. Now he *had* lost time. Five days. But the lapse supported the credibility of his memories. No way he could have lain here that long without being found.

A long list of unanswered messages beeped up on his phone, most from Depaglio and their boss. Braden started to call McCleary but stopped himself. He had no idea how to explain his absence.

He called Depaglio.

"Jesus, Bill, where have you been? The chief has the whole force looking for you."

"I needed some time, Jerry."

"And you don't tell anyone? McCleary's gonna have your ass."

William remembered Yoshiro asking him what he wanted. He walked back toward the stairwell.

"I'll see him in the morning. Don't tell him I called."

"Bill—"

"I'm sorry I worried people. Call it a mid-life crisis."

"They could pull your shield for this."

"Well, if that happens it happens. There's something I need to do."

The phone was silent a moment.

"You all right?" Depaglio asked.

I do not know, Braden thought, but he said, "I'm fine."

"Anything I can help with?"

"Naw, I'm good. Thanks for being a pal." Braden clicked off.

The attendant frowned as Braden passed his booth on street level. Braden waved. He heard the man call after him but ignored him. He retraced the route he'd taken chasing Slick and returned to the Townsley Arms.

The barricades had been removed. Cars and pedestrians passed freely up and down the street. Braden went to the apartment building, rang the buzzer and flashed his badge through the glass. The doorman let him in.

"Top floor," Braden said, going straight toward the elevator bay.

"Of course, detective," the doorman said solicitously, behind him.

Braden had ridden up by himself the first time, too, dreading what he would find. Now that dread was gone. He was angry, determined to find something, anything that would point him in a direction. "A process of discovery," Yoshiro had said. Braden wasn't going to wander around hunting for fucking fairies.

Everything left traces. Dark magic, supernatural experiments—something might have been missed. They hadn't known what they were looking for. Neither did he, but he knew it could be something he might have overlooked five days ago. Investigative experience trained one to question easy assumptions, not the nature of reality. Now he knew to mistrust conventional logic. He wouldn't assume a thing.

He hesitated at the door. His career was already on the rocks. The next thing he was about to do might bury it. He opened the pen knife on his key ring and cut through the FBI seal on the door jamb. He tried the knob. The door wasn't locked.

He turned on the hall lights. The long sofa under the painting that he'd thought might be a Monet was dimly illumed. Braden closed the door behind him.

The chairs around the dining table were positioned as they'd been with the victims seated in them. Fingerprint powder was broadly in evidence. Braden walked slowly around the table. Nothing stopped him.

He did a careful circuit of the living room, then stood in the middle, turning slowly in place, scrutinizing every surface, every object, remembering how it had been. Again, nothing stopped him.

The room at the end of the interior hall that had been locked was open. He turned on the light. Two leather-upholstered armchairs faced utilitarian tables with computers on them. The room was messy with toys, divided, right and left, in type. Nerf gun, football, soccer balls, Transformer models and more Star Wars paraphernalia on the left, stuffed animals, dolls, toy musical instruments, and a building-block fairy tale castle on the right.

Playroom, locked not because of the toys. The parents had restricted their kids' internet access. Monitored them. Braden wouldn't have faulted them for that.

He remembered seeing books in both of the children's rooms. They'd wanted their kids to read books. Real books with physical pages they could hold in their hands.

Braden went to the boy's room, crouched in front of the shelves. The books were carefully arranged, their spines neatly aligned. No fingerprint powder. The investigating team hadn't examined them. Kipling, Stevenson, Tolkien—a long row of Science Fiction. One volume was upside down. *Great Expectations*, by Charles Dickens.

The books in the little girl's room weren't as neat. Kid's picture books, mostly, but not all. *The Wind in the Willows*; Hans Christian Anderson. Not books the girl had read, more likely that her parents had read to her. *Grimm's Fairy Tales* was upside down. Braden got a couple of tissues from the bathroom and carefully extracted the volume. An old book with an elaborately ornate cover. He knelt on one knee and opened it on the floor. One page was dog-eared at the bottom, the title page of "The Juniper Tree." He flipped the folded corner back and forth. He didn't think the girl had done that.

He read the beginning of the story—a dark tale involving the murder of a child. You couldn't get away from the violence of the world, not even in a book of fairy tales.

Something in the atmosphere changed. Braden's head came up. He heard a faint sound, like a sheet of paper scooted along a table by a transient breeze. He stood up and stepped silently to the door, peeked out, looking toward the living room. Nothing. He heard the sound again, to the right. Goosebumps scaled his flesh when he saw a tall, hooded figure in the doorway of the children's playroom.

William had turned off the lights when he left the playroom; the room was dark behind the figure. The person couldn't have entered from the front of the apartment or William would have noticed him. The only other possibility was that he was in the presence of yet another member of the weird clan of the Quick.

William couldn't see the man's face. He wasn't like Slick, nor like Yoshiro or the presiding monk at the temple. A tremendous force emanated from him, like the blast of a jet engine that produced neither heat nor turbulence but a focused radiation of presence.

The man stepped forward and William saw him better. He wore long red robes, embroidered with symbols in gold and black, and he carried a tall staff with a triumvirate cross at its apex. William had been wrong about the hood. The man wore a red, oblong hat, like a bishop's mitre, trimmed in gold. His face was long and deeply creased.

"William Braden," the person said in a cavernous voice, "you seek entrance to the school."

Braden reached for his gun, remembered he'd left it at Yoshiro's. He backed from the doorway as the man advanced and turned to face him, barring exit from the girl's room. William had brought down men twice his size and led them away in handcuffs. He had no illusions that he was a match for this one.

The man was waiting for him to respond. "I don't understand," William said.

"Understanding comes with experience."

"I don't know anything about a school."

"You seek understanding. To acquire it you must enter the school."

Braden swallowed. "Who—who are you?"

"I am Cabal, Hierophant of the Labyrinth of Souls."

William backed away until his legs met the girl's bed. He sat down. All the criminals he'd chased, some whom he'd killed out of necessity, to defend his life or others'—here was one he could not identify as friend or foe. But the question he could not frame, that lived at the heart of loss, called out. No person or circumstance he had ever encountered had presented the possibility of an answer. Not until now.

William knew he was at a threshold. If he stepped forward, he would leave behind the life he knew, for all its pains and frustrations favored with familiarity. And he might never return.

"Let's—let's say I agree—" he lifted his hand in a forestalling gesture—"hypothetically. What will happen to me?"

"That is unknowable. First you must give me your coin." The Hierophant extended his left hand.

William frowned. He patted his pockets, fished out the coin the monk had given him. "This?"

Cabal nodded.

William looked at the coin. On one side it was inscribed with a sword, its blade upturned through a levitating crown, on the other with an eye encircled by a laurel wreath. William sighed and held out the coin.

"It is required that you place it in my palm," Cabal said.

William didn't want to stand. He was tired and his mind ached from too much bewilderment. "Come here and I will."

Cabal remained outside the door with his hand extended. He meant William to go to him. William relaxed his arm and let it rest on his knee, hand dangling, coin between forefinger and thumb.

People who made you go to them always wanted something. It was a power move, like holding your hand low so someone had to bow to shake it. The perception roused William's mistrust.

"You're making this all about me. What do you get out of it? What's so important about this coin?"

"The coin is a symbol. It has the power to bind you to your intention."

"That's one question answered. I asked two."

Cabal lowered his hand. "William Simon Braden, son, grandson, and great-grandson of officers of law, first of your line to waken to the Quick. The women of your line devoted themselves to their spouses, and you esteem them greatly, yet you have never bonded with a woman yourself."

William straightened. "You know a hell of a lot about me, and I don't know a damn thing about you."

"You hated your father for his treatment of your mother. It angers you even now."

Braden stood up. "You're starting to piss me off, too."

"You fear, because of deeds you have witnessed and deeds you have done, that you might behave as your father before you, and so lead a solitary existence."

William gritted his teeth, glaring at the Hierophant.

"You stand in the quarters of a child who was violated beyond the measures of the flesh. This threshold I will not cross."

William advanced a step, holding up the coin. "I give you this, you going to help me catch the bastard who violated her?"

"No."

"Then what the hell good are you? Maybe I'll just hang onto it."

"If you do, you will have no chance of apprehending the perpetrator yourself."

William stepped closer. "There's things you're not saying, and you want something from me."

"What I desire is of no consequence." The Hierophant again extended his hand.

"Yeah, right." More out of frustration than decisiveness, William strode forward and slapped the coin in the Hierophant's palm. It was like plonking it down on a headstone. Hand, arm, body—the Hierophant was steady as granite.

"Behold," Cabal said softly. Heat emanated from his hand. William stepped back as the coin turned red hot, then white, and melted into the weird being's skin. With a faint wisp of smoke, the coin was gone, leaving the skin of Cabal's palm unmarred.

William swallowed. "What now?"

Cabal reached into his robe and pulled out a gun in a rolled-up shoulder holster, handed the items to William.

William pulled the Glock 19 out of its holster. The scratches and wear marks were unmistakable. The gun was his. "How the hell …

"You will have need of it."

William ejected the clip, which was full, and confirmed that the chamber was empty. He re-holstered the weapon, took off his jacket, strapped on the shoulder holster and pulled his jacket back on.

"Come," Cabal said, and proceeded down the hall.

William followed him through the living room into the dining room. The lights in the latter came on without either of them touching a switch. Cabal pointed to the chair where the little girl had died.

"Sit there."

William hesitated. He had an instinct that this was going someplace he wouldn't like, but he stepped around the table and sat down.

Cabal fanned the fingers of his right hand through the air between them and said, "Know her pain."

William convulsed in agony, slammed his head on the table and recoiled backwards, gasping for breath. Cold lava seared his lungs; insects of acid swarmed through his body. The violation went deeper, into his mind, his memory, penetrating the ineffable part of him that was not flesh, defiling it all, mangling, rending, scrambling the parts. Whimpering in terror, he knew the annihilation of his being.

And William Braden sundered unto death.

Chapter Six

Warmth on his back—a hand, stroking him gently. Humidity. The smell of damp stone. A voice murmuring, "Be at peace. Be at peace. Be at peace."

William blinked his eyes open. He lay on his side, body clenched in a foetal posture. A rock wall came into focus, figures, symbols, letters of the alphabet, carved in relief on its surface. The wall seemed to glow.

He inhaled sharply, like he'd been submerged, gulped air. The terror.

"Gently," the voice said. "Gently."

He breathed. His consciousness coalesced into the self he knew. Panic receded. The terror had passed. Gradually, his muscles relaxed.

He turned his head, seeking the source of the voice. A woman knelt beside him. Her eyes, kind, steady and deep, were a refuge personified, something he'd sought and never known.

He groaned, rolled on his belly, pushed himself to his knees. "Where am I?"

"I do not know."

Braden sat back on his heels, closed his eyes and calmed his breathing. The ordeal he had suffered came back to him and he pushed it from his mind. He could not, would not think about it. Easier to mean than achieve. The memory clawed for attention.

"Am I dead?"

"I do not think so."

Braden absently picked up his hat, put it on and winced. "Not sure?" There was a fair-sized bump on his forehead.

"Not entirely, no."

He saw, then, that she was old and wore a brown habit. "You're a nun."

She smiled. "I am, yes. Of the order of the Carmelites."

Braden didn't know what that was. "How did I get here?"

"I do not know that either. You appeared. Out of a very strange mist."

"Who are you?"

"My name is Beatrice Cloutier."

That seemed to William a lovely name, full of music. "You're a nun."

"I believe we covered that."

"Right. Sorry. How did you get here? Wait—" he sighed, "you don't know."

She smiled and shook her head, helped William to his feet. He liked her smile. It warmed him.

Beatrice took in the person before her. Not a tall man—he had a high, peaked hairline, a faintly cleft chin, and a jaw hardened to the contours of underlying muscle. There was deep tiredness in his eyes. Also kindness. He had endured some ordeal that had shaken him. He kept blinking and stretching his eyes, and there was a tremor in his hand when he touched the bump on his forehead. Nevertheless, Beatrice sensed a steadiness in him that few possessed.

William stared about at the walls. They were carven everywhere, even on the ceiling. "Where the hell—Where are we?"

"It appears to be a kind of archive of symbols. Though it seems more than that."

"Archive?"

"Perhaps more of a reliquary."

William stared at her.

"A reliquary is—"

"I know what a reliquary is."

"Well, look." Beatrice gestured at the near wall. "Each figure, be it the letter of an alphabet, an ideogram, hiero-glyph, pictograph or logosyllabic grapheme, is accompa-nied by an attribution, suggestive of a significant incidence of usage by a specific author. The organization seems random, and the intention contemplative. Possibly."

"Contemplative?"

"I have lived a devotional life. I recognize the ear-marks."

"You mean we're in a kind of church."

"Not exactly. I don't think it's a place of observance or worship, and it doesn't feel like a sanctuary. More a place where efforts to communicate are recorded in a fundamental way. Honored, maybe—something like that."

Braden stepped to the near wall and scrutinized a giant letter 'N,' rendered in relief with precision. There were chisel marks in the surrounding stone. Under the N was the name, Gustave Flaubert. To the N's right, under a giant 'O,' Hildegard von Bingen. A lot of the symbols were from systems William didn't know. "So, what," he pointed to a giant 'C' attributed to Louisa May Alcott, "she made the most important use of this letter?"

"I don't know about most important. Significant in some way. I have found several attributions to the same letters, some rendered in different fonts. And, as you see, there are many different alphabets and symbol systems represented, including some dead ones. I saw Sumerian somewhere." She pointed: "Chinese, Cyrillic, Egyptian hieroglyph. Native American pictograph, I think." She gazed about. "Many I can't identify. It has made me think about language differently."

"How long have you been here?"

"No idea, really. I have slept six or seven times, and I am regular in my habits, so perhaps a week."

"What have you been living off of?"

"I'm not sure about that, either. Something has sustained me. There is water, if you're thirsty."

Braden worked his tongue in his mouth. "I am, yeah."

Beatrice gestured for him to accompany her.

"How big is this place?"

"I have walked a long way in both directions and never encountered an end. It changes, too. The last time I passed this way, you were not here."

"Is there a way out?"

"Not that I have found."

William heard water flowing. Beatrice led him to a spring that issued from about twenty feet up the cavern wall and spilled into a pool. He knelt and drank. The water was cool and crisp. He slaked his thirst and sat back, leaning against a rock.

"So, you've been living off of water for a week."

"I am hungry, to be sure. I'm used to fasting, but I will need solid food at some point. It is curious, though."

"What?"

"How old would you say I am?"

"I don't like to guess about that. People are living longer, these days. I've met some in their seventies who looked in their fifties."

"I'm approaching my ninetieth year."

"You're holding together well."

"Yes, better than when I arrived. Before I came here, I would have described myself to be in an advanced state of decrepitude. My customary posture was quite bent, I moved slowly of necessity, and my memory was failing. Here, as you see, I stand straight, my stride is agile. My mind is clear, too, my memories greatly restored. All this with nothing but water and the atmosphere of this place to rejuvenate me."

Braden looked both ways down the cavern. "Where's the light come from, the walls?"

"It seems so."

"Does it ever get dark?"

"Not since I have been here."

"I'm guessing you've been reluctant to stray too far from this spring."

"I confess that is so. I have found no other water source in my explorations."

"We're going to have to find a way out of here, or we'll starve."

Beatrice smiled. "I may be braver with a companion."

William liked the old gal. She was straight, and she had guts. He was glad not to be alone himself. He pointed up at an inscription above the spring. "Can you read that?"

"It's the only one I've seen with graphemes combined to make a word. At least I think it's a word. I have studied Sanskrit a little, but I am not well-versed. At a guess it might mean 'source,' or possibly 'way.' It's also the only one I've seen without an attribution."

William considered the waterfall, a glassy sheet about eight feet wide. It was darker in the center than it was to either side.

He took off his hat, jacket, gun, shoes and socks, caught Beatrice eyeing the gun.

"I'm a cop," he said.

"I ascertained that."

He twisted his lips, rolled up his sleeves. He stepped around the pool to the edge of the waterfall and thrust his hand through the spilling water.

Beatrice watched him. Not one given to hesitation was William Braden, nor readily to distraction. His mind and body moved in unison, from one task or question to the next, riding the boat of time with purpose, ignoring his pains and the share of burdens he bore in his soul. She understood these things about him without knowing how. She recognized them the way one might a familiar land-scape.

William felt about through the waterfall, encountered no hard surface. He climbed into the pool, took a deep breath and poked his head through.

He withdrew and pushed his hair back. "There's a passage," he told Beatrice. "Cramped, but it looks pass-able."

"How did I ever miss that?"

"I'm glad you did, or I would have woken up here alone. Shall we give it a try?"

"Certainly."

William wrapped his gun and Slick's E-fit in his hat, wrapped that and his shoes in his jacket. Beatrice hiked up her skirt and tied it off.

They waded into the pool together, William holding Beatrice's hand. William threw his wrapped-up jacket and its contents through the waterfall, then helped Beatrice up into the passage beyond.

The way was narrow and dimly illumined. William pulled his shoes, holster and jacket back on. He held Slick's E-fit in his hand to keep it dry as possible and proceeded down the passage with Beatrice close behind. Past the first bend they entered total darkness. William reached for Beatrice's hand, found it, and they felt their way along. Some distance on they detected light ahead.

William stopped. "Do you smell that?"

Beatrice sniffed. "Smells like … the sea!"

William grinned. Beatrice's features acquired youth, softened in the dimness. He could see that she was smiling, too. She had maybe the warmest smile he'd seen on a woman.

They arrived at the mouth of the passage, which was obstructed by vines of some sort. Braden pushed through and held Beatrice's hand as she followed.

They arrived on the shore of an underworld ocean bordered by jungle in a cavern vast as a world. Far out on the water, ships from a bygone era sailed.

Chapter Seven

Dense jungle, crowded with vegetation the likes of which neither Beatrice nor William had ever seen, flanked them on their right as they walked along a beach of blue-streaked white sand. The ceiling of the cavern was hazy and vague in the high distances above; out across the water its end could not be seen.

Fronds of low, ground-hugging creepers uncurled as they passed, seeming to reach for them from the fringe of vegetal growth. Animate, lacy flowers, too, strained towards the journeyers. They saw sprawling plants with leaves the size of beach umbrellas, multi-hued like a painter's fantasy; delicate vines, peppered with tiny crimson flowers, that spiraled around any stem or branch; ferns tall as palm trees with turquoise fronds—the diversity of the jungle seemed endless. There were no trees, but giant mushrooms with broad trunks and massive caps stood thirty and more feet tall.

"We've been silent a long while," Beatrice observed.

"My mind's on pause."

"Yes, mine too. Where is the light coming from?"

"Everywhere, I think. Look at your shadow."

Beatrice looked down. Her shadow, pale and faint, extended from her like an encircling fan. "It's like a dream."

"We ain't asleep." William pointed at the ships on the water. "There's a port ahead, somewhere."

"What sort of people do you imagine live here?"

"We're going to have to find out."

A distance along they heard sounds of chopping and sawing. The noise grew as they drew abreast of it.

"Through there." William stepped into the jungle.

Beatrice followed him through the dense, high foliage. Some of the plants clung to her as she pressed along.

William put his arm out, stopping her. He pointed.

A crew of men were chopping down giant mushrooms, while others stripped their trunks and fashioned them into planks. The huge, concentrically multi-hued caps were stacked up around their work area.

Beatrice and William withdrew from the scene. When they returned to the beach, they met a tall, heavily bearded man waiting for them. His garments, pants and blouse, were loose and unpleated, secured at the waist with a broad belt. Pushed under the belt was the handle of a sharp-looking adze.

"Help you folks?"

Beatrice realized that William was not going to answer. The men were sizing each other up the way men did. "We don't know our way around here," she said.

The man frowned at her, hands on hips, glanced back and forth between her and William. "You two are fresh off the concrete, aren't you?"

Neither Beatrice nor William knew how to respond.

The man laughed, shaking his head. "Didn't know old dogs had the wits." He pointed up the beach. "Little ways along you'll run into Keel."

"That's a town?" William asked.

"It is. I'm guessing you two might be hungry."

"We are, yes," Beatrice said.

"Look for a tavern by the harbor called the Glass Toad. Ask for Peat. Tell him Bristol sent you. He'll feed you."

"That's very kind, thank you," Beatrice said. Bristol nodded and plunged into the jungle, laughing and shaking his head as he went.

The lay of the land acquired a steepening grade as they continued on. Around a bend in the coastline they encountered dwellings, nestled in the dense flora. Past a sloping ridgeline they entered the town of Keel, where unpainted, plank-walled buildings with shake-shingle roofs scaled the topography to the limit of the cavern wall.

The denizens of the town were all dressed in plain, simple garments similar to Bristol's. Many of the men wore tri-corner hats. The women mostly wore long skirts and either had their hair tied back or gathered in loose-woven snoods. Near the harbor the bustle of activity increased. Beatrice and William attracted attention, moving among the rest. Most of those they passed smiled and nodded in a friendly fashion. Many eyed them with curiosity.

The ships at anchor were all sailing vessels, many quite large with three masts. The Glass Toad faced the harbor. William noted that the unpainted walls of the exterior had no grain. He stroked the door jamb as he went inside. Smooth, like finished pine.

Square-topped tables and straight-backed chairs occupied the floor space, cushionless booths lining the water-side wall beneath a line of mullioned windows. A dozen or so patrons sat eating and drinking. On the opposite side of the tavern was an L-shaped bar. A balding, bespectacled person stood behind it, wiping the counter.

William and Beatrice approached him.

"We're looking for Peat," William said. "Bristol sent us."

The man, bending to sort things under the counter, didn't look at them. "Don't know him. Peat's not here. Back tomorrow." On a high shelf behind him rested a blown-glass flagon in the shape of frog, the mouth of which formed the vessel's brim. The frog was full of coins.

William glanced at Beatrice. "We'd like something to eat."

The man nodded. "Fish stew's two croppers. Ale's a 'hacropper more."

William took out his wallet. "All I've got is US currency." He pulled out a few bills and held them out to the barkeep.

The man finally looked at them. His eyebrows rose. "Anyone going upside?" he called across the bar. "Guy needs to exchange some American money."

No one answered. The barkeep grinned helplessly. "Sorry."

"Is there a bank?"

"Not in Keel. Might try the shops or ask around the harbor."

"I'll cover them," a voice said.

William and Beatrice turned. A very short, heavily bearded man sitting alone at a table near the center of the room smiled and waved them over.

"Join me. Please."

They went to his table and sat down.

"Thanks," William said. "I'll get you back soon as I can change some money."

"You'll find that difficult. Most of the townspeople were born here and don't much travel. You've just come from upside, haven't you?"

"If by 'upside' you mean the surface of the planet Earth, yeah," William answered.

"Let's introduce ourselves. I'll begin. I am Gan Altum, captain of the *Passenger*, currently at anchor just there." He pointed through a window.

Beatrice and William looked and saw a large, fat-bellied vessel, ship-rigged with three masts.

"You're the captain?" William failed to mask his surprise.

"You think a dwarf can't be a captain?" Gan asked.

William grimaced and cleared his throat in embarrassment.

Gan chuckled. "Don't worry, it's a common reaction. Used to be, at any rate. Now tell me who you are."

William and Beatrice introduced themselves.

"And you're new here?"

"Yeah, about that—where, exactly, is 'here?'" William asked.

"That's a difficult question to answer in a way likely to make much sense to you. You're in a stable part of the Labyrinth, which is connected to the Earth in a way I'm not competent to explain. All I can tell you is that the connection is inter-dependent. Without Earth, this place wouldn't exist. I'm not sure the reverse is true. I'm told there's a map in Crystalon that clarifies things, somewhat, but I've never seen it."

"If you can't tell us *where* here is, how about *what* here is?"

Gan laughed. "Even harder to answer, I'm afraid. It has something to do with the collective effects of consciousness."

William sighed. "Well, that clears it up."

The barkeep brought their food. William regarded the thick, dark 'stew' in the bowl placed before him with uncertainty.

"Let's have some bread, too, Homer," Gan said.

"Ale?"

"Yes, and fruit. Whatever you have."

William sniffed the stew. It smelled meaty and good, but he couldn't identify its components. Beatrice was less hesitant. She made the sign of the cross, closed her eyes and murmured a short prayer, then delivered a spoonful to her mouth and chewed. Her face lit up. She swallowed and said, "That's wonderful."

William cocked a skeptical eye at her. Everything tasted good when you were hungry. He sipped from his spoon. The rich mixture of flavors that bloomed in his mouth banished doubt. He scooped up a spoonful. The fish was denser than any he'd eaten before, but pleasant to chew. There was a heavy flavor of mushrooms, and vegetables unknown to him. The overall effect was a joy to the palate. "That's all right," William said. He and Beatrice focused on eating.

William tore a piece off a dark, brown bun and mopped up the residue in the bowl. The bread tasted of mushrooms, too. He took a long drink of ale and belched. Beatrice and Gan laughed.

William smacked his lips with satisfaction. "That most definitely did not suck."

"How did you come to the Labyrinth, Sister?" Gan asked Beatrice. "That is the correct way to address a nun, is it not?"

"Yes, but you may call me Beatrice." She related how she had arrived in the Labyrinth.

"That's a remarkable tale," Gan said. "So why are you here?"

"I have no idea."

"Really. Well, you can be sure there is a reason. People never make the crossing without one."

"I suppose I am here to learn something. I began with a question. Perhaps I will find an answer."

Gan regarded her thoughtfully. He turned to William. "And you?"

"I'm looking for this guy." William unfolded the E-fit of Slick, passed it to Gan and watched his reaction.

Gan's expression darkened as he viewed the image. "Why?"

"'Cause he's a murdering son-of-a-bitch. Sorry, Beatrice."

"Who did he kill?" Gan asked.

William glanced at Beatrice. She had become somber as well.

"You will not shock me, William."

"Four people," William told Gan. "Parents and their kids."

"He killed children?"

"Little boy was ten, the girl five. I was chasing him in New York, and he jumped—quickened, as you say—to Tokyo. I got sucked after him, somehow. Subsequently a Buddhist monk helped me quicken back to New York. I was investigating the murders when this Cabal character showed up."

"The Hierophant?"

"You know him?"

"I've encountered him."

"He and I are going to have a talk, next we meet. He's the one who sent me—" William spread his hands—"here."

Gan studied the picture of Slick. "How did he kill the family?"

William shook his head. "You don't want to know."

Gan folded the E-fit and gave it back to William. Silence stretched between the three.

William looked around at the walls, rubbed the table-top. "Is this mushroom wood?" he asked, seeking to change the subject.

Gan remained in silent reflection a moment before responding. "It is. Keel is famous for its mushrooms. The trunks are used for lumber. The soft, inner parts of the caps are edible and quite nutritious. You've just eaten some. Anything left over is pulped for paper and fabric."

William shook his head in amazement. "I feel like I've gone back in time, here."

"People from upside often have that impression, when they first come here. You'll find it less true in other parts of the Labyrinth."

"Does everyone speak English?"

"No." Gan mustered a smile. "In the Labyrinth people understand each other."

"What does that mean? You speak it."

"In fact I do not. My primary language is not one spoken on Earth. I was born in the Labyrinth. I have never been upside."

"You're not making sense. You're speaking English clear as day."

Gan waved his hand in contradiction. "I know it seems that way but I'm not. A psychologist of sorts explained it to me once. He described an auditory phenomenon. If you don a certain listening apparatus—headphones I think you call them—is that right, for listening to music?"

William nodded.

"Yes, well, with that apparatus it is possible to isolate what one hears in one ear from what one hears in the other. If you play a certain tone on one side, and a different tone on the other, the mind, seeking equilibrium, invents a third tone, that you 'hear' in your mind, between the other two. Right now, you hear me speaking your primary language very clearly, and I hear you speaking mine. Your mind invents the impression that my lips are moving in agreement with the words you hear. That, at least, was the psychologist's conjecture. If you overhear a conversation that does not involve you, you'll see the difference immediately. If they're not speaking English, or any secondary language you've learned, you won't understand them."

William looked at Beatrice. "But you speak English, right?"

She smiled with her eyebrows raised. "Actually, I've been quite impressed by your facility with French."

"I'll be god damned."

"I certainly hope not." Beatrice glanced around. "Is there a toilet?"

"Through the kitchen." Gan pointed to an entry by the bar.

William watched her go. Her attitude towards him had changed when he'd talked about the murders. He hoped he hadn't alienated her.

He turned to Gan. "You recognized him."

Gan nodded grimly.

"Know where I can find him?"

"I might."

"Where?"

"Minuslitore. But knowing the name of the city won't help you. You don't yet know how to quicken and may need awhile to learn. I ship out in the morning. I'll take you there. You'll have to share my cabin. The passenger berths are taken, and I've got a full crew. I'm guessing you don't know much about sailing."

"Nothing whatsoever."

"You can help load and unload. Fair?"

"Fair enough. But I'm not leaving Beatrice behind."

Gan sighed. "I'll bunk with my crew. The two of you can have my cabin."

"Not meaning to seem unappreciative, why are you so ready to help me?"

Gan fixed on William. "That person does not have friends. I don't think he wants any. But people fear him and may be reluctant to help you. I can't abide someone who hurts children."

"Yeah, I'm sensing a personal grievance."

Gan shrugged. "He cheats at cards."

William grunted. "And you *don't* fear him?"

"I'm a dwarf. I was born with a reason to fear everyone."

"Nevertheless, you're a fucking captain."

"Very perceptive, Detective."

Chapter Eight

Gan secured a room for them in a nearby inn, then left to make preparations for the voyage. William and Beatrice went for a walk along the waterfront in the deepening twilight. Hosts of small fishing boats were at anchor in the harbor, now, along with the larger ships.

William noted the fading light without comment, relieved that some form of night and day existed in this place.

Beatrice stopped, looking out across the water, then up at the diminishingly luminous heights. "All our lives," she said.

"What?" William admired the dignity with which she held her head raised. In that moment, pale blue light limning and softening her features, he was not sure he had ever seen anyone more beautiful. She wore her years like triumphs.

"All our lives, we see things from one perspective— our own, each to our own. Some aspects in common. In times past the world was flat, rode the back of a turtle, the entire universe was held aloft in the hands of a giant man.

Now there are some who believe that the universe came from nothing and is returning inexorably to that self-same state. They mask their panic and desperation when they pretend that that is not the death of meaning."

"You don't think they're right?"

"No."

"Doesn't scare you that they might be?"

"No."

"So, the scientists are wrong."

"No. I understand their perspective. They provide us with valuable information. We are in the same situation with the universe that we are with ourselves. We don't know where we came from, why we are here, or where we are going."

"Not a perspective I'd expect from a nun."

"I did not undergo a lobotomy when I took my vows."

William chuckled. "I guess not."

"But here, in this place, is a very different perspective."

"That is for sure."

They walked down to the water. Low waves lapped quietly against the shore. The ships creaked and swayed at anchor.

"You still have faith?" William asked.

"I admit I am struggling a bit with what that is, at present—faith. But ..."

"What?"

"Imagination. I find comfort in the human imagination. It's the most God-like attribute we have. It is bigger than belief, bigger than knowledge, bigger than certainty, and bigger than fear. Whatever is discovered, the imagination is always bigger, and nothing is ever discovered without it." She looked up at the cavern heights again. "We have not asked all of the questions, and we have not found all of the answers."

"But you still believe in God?"

She turned to him without answering. "What will you do, William, when you find the man you hunt?"

He didn't want to say, tried to get away with, "You know."

"No, I don't. I am a good judge of character. You are not a brutal man. But you are capable of brutality when presented with a grave wrong."

"Everyone's capable of brutality."

"Perhaps. You avoid my question."

William thrust his hands in his pockets. "You've known me the space of a day and you think you know me."

"I don't."

"Look, I like you, all right? I don't want to give you a bad idea about me."

"I like you too, William," Beatrice said softly. "And I would like to know what you're thinking." She watched him stride away. He stopped in front of a bench and sat down facing the water. He was in conflict with himself.

She was asking him to think about things he didn't want to think about until the decision was right in front of him.

She waited for the intensity to lessen between them, then stepped over slowly and sat beside him.

"I know what you're asking," he said in a calmer voice.

She waited, letting him find his own way. There were lights on the water, too, ships at anchor farther out.

William fed a cigarette to his mouth, lit it and crumpled the empty pack. "My dad—" he took a drag, leaned his head back and blew smoke—"in a lot of ways he was a good man. But he was a mean drunk. He'd get a load on, come home and take it out on my mom. He was a big guy, good deal bigger than I am. Fists like bricks. I was afraid of him, until one night I figured out that, if I could swing a bat at a ball, I could just as easily swing it at his head." He didn't see Beatrice wince, but he felt it.

"Did you kill him?'

William shook his head, blowing smoke. "Man had a skull like an iron bunker. But after that he left my mom alone." He took another drag. "Though I'm not sure *she* ever really forgave me."

"That is sad."

"Sister, who I am says a man crosses my sights hurts a child or a woman, I will find that person and hurt him back. Most of my life I've let the legal system do the hurting for me, with varied effectiveness. That guy didn't just kill those kids, they suffered the torments of the damned. He did a rabbit from New York to Tokyo in a hot second. Say I catch him, and somehow get him back to New York. Do you think there's a jail or a prison on Earth that can hold someone like that?"

Beatrice nodded. "I understand." She stood up. "I am tired." She walked, at a ruminative pace, back towards the inn.

William fell in beside her. "Me too."

They climbed the narrow, creaking steps to their small room without speaking. William rolled up his hat, stuck it in a jacket pocket, and folded his jacket over the only chair in the room. He rolled up his gun in his shoulder holster and placed it on the floor by his shoes. Then he lay down on the small cot on the right side of the room and faced the wall to give Beatrice privacy.

She moved about quietly, knelt and murmured her prayers in French. The oil lamp went out and he heard her lie down.

"Good night, William."

"Good night, Beatrice."

The events of the long day rustled through William's mind like a disorganized parade of exotic animals. He could not make sense of them in any way that accommodated understanding. He did not know how to evaluate or examine them. He could only watch them drift and mill.

At the liminal edge of sleep the horror came back to him, what the young girl had gone through, being torn apart body and being, all she had known and felt and remembered savagely divided into smaller and smaller parts, scrambled until they were deprived of any semblance of coherence.

Perversely, rather than keep him from sleep, the awful memories pulled him into it. What he experienced then could not be defined as either dream or awareness. He entered a dimensionless vastness of dismembered psyches, fragments and particles of selves churning together in a lost state, desperate to reclaim individuation, rendering themselves more ruined by their efforts, thrashing and roiling in a common condition of horror and despair, reaching, reaching, unable to hold anything.

Deep, deep in that chaotic maelstrom, William detected a presence, a single unified consciousness so malevolent and destructive it surpassed his comprehension. No name, no comparison, was equal to its nature. To call it evil was not only inadequate but meaningless. William was drawn toward the presence, helpless to resist.

He awakened with a shout, not knowing where he was. He threw his legs over the edge of the bed and sat up, shivering, soaked in sweat.

Beatrice sat on her bed, watching him. In the strange pale light of the labyrinthine night, her silver hair, flowing over her shoulders, seemed to glow. Her eyes, flecked with a faint blue gleam, were a sanctuary. William again saw something in them he had looked for and lost, without ever having found it, a truth he had doubted and needed and hoped for: a quiet, calm grace, gentle as a feather.

"You are all right, William."

"I don't think I am."

She reached out and placed her hand on his, and he couldn't keep from breaking down. She moved next to him on his bed, and he fell against her, weeping, taking shelter in her warmth. "It was a phantasm," she said.

"No, it was real. Oh, my God, Sister. Oh, my God."

"Shh, shh, you are safe. I am here." She stroked his head and his back and held him until he quieted. She helped him lie back down and pulled the blanket over him. "Sleep, now. Sleep peacefully. I will watch over you. You are under my protection."

In that moment, William fell in love with Beatrice. If anyone would have mocked him for it, they would have received a swift teaching.

❧

When William awoke, daylight was filtering through the thin curtains. Beatrice was gone. Her habit lay neatly folded on her bed.

William found a small washroom down the corridor and freshened himself as he could. He longed for a razor and a toothbrush.

He went downstairs and out into the narrow, cobbled street. He didn't see Beatrice, so he headed towards the harbor, found Gan overseeing the loading of the *Passenger*.

Gan cocked an impatient eye when he saw William coming. "You're late."

"I don't even know how to tell time, here! There wasn't a clock in the room."

Gan pointed at his own head. "The clock's in here. Use it."

Incredulous, William laughed. "Is Beatrice on board?"

Gan gestured up the pier behind William.

She wore a plain, brown peasant dress, now, tied at the waist with a cord. Her long, silver hair caught the flow of the ocean breeze. She carried a basket on her arm. She smiled her warming smile at William. She still bore all the facial weathering of old age but seemed indefinably younger than she had the day before.

She held out the basket. "I thought you might be hungry."

The things in the basket were all unfamiliar. William couldn't tell if they were fruits or vegetables.

Beatrice chuckled at his uncertainty. She plucked a string-bean looking thing that was bluish in color from the basket and held it up to his mouth. "Try this."

William gave her a skeptical look. He opened his mouth and she popped it in. His eyes widened when he bit down. It was crunchy but it tasted like a blueberry.

He chewed with pleasure and swallowed. "Okay, you won me."

"These are plum-like in flavor," she said, pointing at something that looked like a red avocado, "and these more like apples." The latter looked like a small, purple, crook-necked squash. "I don't really know how to describe these—" she pointed at a round, spiny, yellow fruit—"but they're my favorite. They're tart. You can eat the skin. Here," she gave him the basket, "take them with you."

"Gan says we're late. We have to get on board."

Beatrice picked up a draw-string bag from the pier beside her. "He gave me money to get you some things. There's a change of clothes. He said your street clothes won't do, on board. And I picked up some other essentials for you. I hope you know how to use a straight razor."

"I'll manage." William accepted the bag. "Thanks. Come on." He leaned toward the ship.

Beatrice's smile faded. "I'm not going with you, William."

"What?" It hit him like a blow. He could see that her mind was made up. He couldn't hide his disappointment, didn't try.

Beatrice was surprised by the depth of his reaction but met it impassively. He was a grown man and she respected him. She trusted him to contend with his feelings. Nevertheless, seeing him so affected caused a tightening in her chest. She hadn't realized how attached to William she had become in their short time together.

"What will you do?" he asked.

"I don't know. I need time to find myself again and understand what I'm doing here."

"You can't do that with us?" He leaned toward the ship again.

She held his gaze and didn't answer.

He sighed. "This is about me, isn't it? What I'm doing."

"I understand what you're doing, William. I won't even argue that it's wrong. But I can't be a part of it."

William looked down the harbor, chewing his lip. "I get that." He hoisted the sack up under his arm. "I'm worried about you being on your own."

"I'll be fine."

"Of course you will. Course you will."

They stood a moment in awkward silence.

"Thanks for last night," he said, "and everything."

"You are very welcome. And thank you."

He shrugged. "I didn't do anything."

She put a hand on his face and made him look at her. "You're a good man, William Braden."

Old or not, nun or not, he wanted to take her in his arms.

"I wish you good fortune. I will pray for you."

William watched Beatrice walk away, feeling like he ought to go after her, and not knowing how to.

Chapter Nine

Boarding the ship, William felt even more that he had gone back in time. The crew, male and female, all wore breeches gathered at the knees and loose-fitting tunics with wide, elbow-length sleeves. Some wore scarves on their heads, others tri-corner hats. The sailors were a rugged lot. William wouldn't have liked to tangle with any of them. He asked a tall, bulky fellow toting a barrel on his shoulder the way to the captain's cabin. The man pointed at a door atop a flight of stairs under the sterncastle.

William climbed the steps and entered the cabin. The compartment was larger than he would have expected, centered by a long table and several chairs. A large, mullioned window opened across the back of the space. To the left was a built-in bed, to the right a desk and shelves of books. Beside the desk was an entry to a well-appointed head.

A folded collapsible cot leaned against the stern beside the window. William wondered when he might sleep in a real bed again.

He took in the view through the window, watched people mill along the harbor front. Such a strange reality he had entered.

He changed into the clothes Beatrice had bought for him. The leather-soled boots were a little snug but mostly everything fit well enough. William looked at himself in the mirror. Beatrice had provided a woven cap, as well. William decided to stick with his pork pie hat.

He went back out on deck and looked for a way to make himself useful. For the next couple of hours, he helped load cargo and provisions on board. He was embarrassed by how weak he was compared to his shipmates, but no one said anything.

When the loading was done, he slaked his thirst from a water barrel on the main deck and poured a ladle full over his head.

Gan came up the ramp and grinned at him. He signaled, and William followed him to a bench under the forecastle. He passed William a flask. William drank. He let the whisky wash around in his mouth before swallowing.

"Thanks. I needed that."

"Eases the muscles." Gan packed tobacco into a white, clay pipe with a small bowl and a long stem, patted his pockets.

William gave him his lighter.

"Thank you." Gan lit the pipe.

William watched him smoke. "Wish I had a cigarette."

"I have an extra pipe."

Gan crossed the deck and climbed the stairs to his cabin. While he was gone, William watched three of the strangest people he had ever seen board the ship. One was a hulking giant of a man dressed like a cowboy in chaps and a leather vest. He had to be eight feet tall without the ten-gallon hat. William noted the revolvers holstered at his waist. He was followed by an enormously obese woman who lounged on a levitating divan. William couldn't see how the divan stayed aloft, especially with her on it. The thing seemed to carry her where she wanted to go.

Strange as those two were, the next person to come aboard made William rise to his feet in astonishment. Not only did he wear no clothing, aside from a belt with a scabbard for a long, slim knife, he had no skin. The veins and sinews of his body were entirely exposed to view. He caught William staring at him and responded with what might have been a smile.

"Archetypes," Gan said, returning to the bench.

William watched the skinless man enter a cabin and close the door. "What?" He sat back down.

Gan packed the second pipe and gave it to William. "Archetypes. Persons who have had the misfortune to be altered by the Labyrinth to serve an arcane purpose."

"Am I supposed to understand that?" William put the stem of the pipe to his lips and Gan lit it for him.

"This tobacco is strong," Gan said. "If you're going to inhale, take small puffs."

William, preoccupied with bewilderment, wasn't listening. He inhaled and coughed explosively.

"I warned you."

William recovered from the coughing fit and wiped tears from his eyes. "Jesus." He took another pull from Gan's flask. "How can a guy live with no skin?"

"Uncomfortably, I should imagine. Why don't you ask him? Pellis is quite personable and not easily offended."

"That's his name?"

Gan nodded.

The giant came out of his cabin, crossed the main deck, and climbed to the deck of the forecastle. William couldn't keep from staring as he went by.

"Archetypes."

"That's what we call them," Gan said. "As I understand it, every so often someone from upside—from the world you know—crosses into the Labyrinth and undergoes a change. For some it only affects their clothing. Whenever they're out amongst others, their clothing changes to what they've become stuck with as archetypes, and they can't do anything about it. For others the transformation is more profound."

"And they can't control it."

"From what I understand, no."

William looked in the direction of Pellis' cabin. "Poor son-of-a-bitch."

"Yes, when I'm frustrated with my own physical circumstances, I sometimes reflect upon his."

"You know him?"

"We've spoken."

"I think I'd find that difficult."

"Many worthwhile things are. Excuse me, it's time to get underway." He left the lighter and his tobacco pouch with William. "Remember, small puffs. Sheply!"

A tall, lanky woman with a blade-like face and skin the color of umber emerged from below decks. "Aye-aye, Captain!"

"Weigh anchor."

William stood port side as the *Passenger* pulled away from Keel. He searched for Beatrice but could not see her.

❖

Beatrice wandered the streets of Keel, taking in the people and the humble, unpainted homes. She climbed to the cavern wall and touched its surface, scrutinized it with curiosity. Up close it appeared simply to be yellowish, composite rock.

She looked out across the town and the sea. The *Passenger* had set sail and was well away from the harbor. Again, Beatrice felt a pull in her chest, and wondered if she should have gone with William. She cast the notion aside. Foolishness. She might have regained a measure of vigor, but she was still an old woman. She had given her life to God. It was too late for anything else.

She watched the ship a long while and prayed for William's safety.

She had no money. She would have to find a way to earn some. She continued her explorations, considering at each shop, each door, if she might have something of worth to offer.

On the outskirts of the town, opposite the end from which she and William had entered, she encountered a woman, white-haired like herself, at work in a large garden. The woman was tilling earth along a row of vines of some kind with a hand trowel. Behind her a steaming iron kettle hung from a raised bar above a small, banked fire.

The woman noticed Beatrice. She stopped her work and leaned back on her haunches. "What's ailing you?"

The question surprised Beatrice. "Nothing, so far as I know."

The woman stood, peering at Beatrice. "I don't know you. Where are you from?"

"I believe you call it 'upside,' here."

It was the woman's turn to be surprised. "When did you cross?"

"I'm not certain exactly but a short while ago. Perhaps a week."

"At your age? Why?"

"I don't know. I arrived in Keel yesterday. I was glad to encounter a town."

The woman wiped her hands on her apron and came to the fence. "You must be experiencing some confusion."

"I am a little, yes."

The woman extended her hand. "Mirabel Glacé."

Beatrice shook her hand and introduced herself.

"I'm sort of the doctor, around here."

"I was admiring your garden. I know none of these plants."

"I can teach you, if you want. I'm preparing some lung and throat powder." She gestured at the cavern heights. "Weather's going to turn, before long. The Jack pollen'll get stirred up and the patients'll be coming. I could use a hand, if you've nothing else to do."

"Certainly. I'm looking for work. I have no money."

"I can use you. I can't pay you much, but I'll keep you fed, make a place for you to stay."

Beatrice smiled. "That would be very agreeable."

Mirabel held the gate open and Beatrice followed her through her garden. Mirabel took the kettle off the fire and set it on a flat stone. "That needs to cool for awhile. Mostly bark fungus and bean berry seeds. The important ingredients are black lace flower and dried glow worms. I'll teach you the mixture." The woman patted the air above the pot. "That's poisonous, right now. We have to treat it to tease out the medicine."

Mirabel led Beatrice on through her garden to a melon patch. The melons were white and round, about the size of cantaloupes but smooth-skinned. They had thread-thin, crooked blue stripes.

"These are ice melons. Not very good to eat but they have other uses." She took a hooked knife from her pocket and cut one of the melons free of the vine. "Everything's got a use. We might not see it, but sure as daylight it's got one." She cut a large hole in the base of the melon. "We need to scoop out the seeds and the meat down to the rind. Dump the guts in those." She pointed to a row of wooden buckets. "They've got other uses."

Mirabel found a second knife, gave it to Beatrice, and the two women worked together. When they had all of the melons scooped out, Mirabel brought the kettle over. In it was a muddy, green paste. She stirred in water to bring it to a liquid state.

"Prop your melon so the hole faces up, then pour in a ladle of the decoction. Swirl it around inside the melon 'til it's well coated and pour what's left back in the pot. Don't get any of the decoction on you." Mirabel demonstrated.

They coated the melons, then Beatrice helped Mirabel carry them to a thatch-roofed shed, and down into a cellar beneath. They hung all the melons by their stems from hooks in the cellar ceiling and left them there.

"Let's take a break," Mirabel said. "I'll fix us something to eat."

She prepared a salad of leafy greens tossed with crumbled cheese, nuts, sliced fruit and a sweet dressing, and warmed up some mushroom bread. They ate at a small white table in Mirabel's cottage. The orderliness and simplicity of the cottage was a comfort to Beatrice. It reminded her of the cloister.

She let Mirabel do most of the talking. She learned that the old healer's husband had died some time back. Clearly, she welcomed someone to talk to. Beatrice also learned something of the ways of the people of Keel, and, in a more random way, about the Labyrinth.

They worked through the afternoon and then Mirabel set up a pallet for Beatrice in a room lined with clay pots full of dried herbs. The room had a wonderful smell and Beatrice slept peacefully.

In the morning, after a breakfast of fruit and hearth bread, they returned to the cellar. A glistening green frost had developed on the surfaces of the melons.

"See, the medicinal properties of the decoction have migrated through the rind, left the poison behind, and taken on the cooling properties of the melon. We need to scrape off the frost and leave it to cure. But first, let me see, yes, here's a little patch that's dry enough." Mirabel took a tiny spoon from her pocket and scraped some powder into it. She held the spoon inside her open mouth and inhaled. "Yep, that's good. Want to try it?"

Beatrice shrugged and nodded.

Mirabel scraped some more powder into the spoon. "Open wide." She held the spoon inside Beatrice's mouth. "Now, inhale sharply."

Beatrice inhaled, sucking the powder from the spoon into her throat. An extraordinary cooling sensation spread through her throat and lungs. Her eyes widened.

Mirabel smiled. "I call it Ice Melon Frost. Any sort of inflammation in your throat or lungs, it'll fix you up."

Beatrice gazed about at the glistening, frost-covered melons, and a nascent understanding awakened in her. The person she had been, the faith she had possessed and nurtured, was migrating through the rind of her psyche towards some yet unperceived purpose. Not an entirely comfortable notion, for it begged the question: what was she losing? But she knew that a purpose existed now, for her, and she would find it.

Chapter Ten

Days aboard the *Passenger* came and went. William busied himself as he could. He looked through Gan's books, all in languages he could not read, some elaborately rendered by hand. A few had pictures—etchings and hand-inked images, some hand-colored. Botanical and zoological illustrations, engrossing and confounding. Life had evolved differently in the Labyrinth. Depictions of seafaring hazards—perilous reefs, roiling storms, fearsome creatures of monstrous proportions. Maps of regions encompassing the waters they traveled increased William's mystification more than clarified his sense of place.

At times it seemed that a faculty with which he was not familiar opened in his mind, and the unintelligible words in one or another of the books became transiently scrutable, as if a language he had forgotten returned to his command. But such experiences were fleeting, and he could not hold what he read.

Whenever they reached a port, William went ashore and showed Slick's E-fit around. Most did not recognize him—the few who William sensed did denied it.

He wanted to converse with the archetypes, but they kept to themselves. Gan told him to just knock on their doors and introduce himself, but William wanted to encounter them casually on deck. He was not easily intimidated. The Hierophant had been the first in a very long while to cow him, and the effect hadn't lasted. But the bizarre circumstances of the archetypes' lives made William uneasy. He did not want to seem too interested— so he told himself. His real reluctance was more primal. He didn't want whatever they had to rub off.

They came, at length, to the port city of High Harbor, at an intersection of caverns that extended beyond sight in several directions. William saw that life in the Labyrinth was much more varied than he had yet experienced. No clusters of wooden shacks, here, but homes of brick and stone, some mansion-like in scale. Around the city spread vast reaches of rolling farmlands and green hills.

There were also steam ships, mammoth dirigibles and other flying crafts both large and small. Wheeled vehicles traveled roadways paved in yellow cobbles that gleamed like polished stone. And yet all of this activity occurred with ethereal quietness, the city producing collectively a low, unobtrusive hum.

Gan accompanied William off of the ship and hired a transport to take them into the city. The workings of the vehicle confounded William. It seemed little more than a glass shell over a chassis with four wheels. There was no hood or trunk, and William couldn't figure out where the motor was. He asked Gan about it.

"My understanding is that it's powered directly by energy drawn from the Labyrinth."

"That's a neat trick."

"I don't really understand the mechanics involved."

"Runs by rubric," the driver said. He was a slim, dark-skinned person with greying hair. "You have to have training. The rig recognizes my nomenclature."

"Did you understand that?" William asked Gan quietly.

Gan shook his head.

William watched people on the streets. They seemed a mix of every kind, and their dress varied greatly. Many wore long robes, others pants, shirts and dresses closer to modes he was accustomed to. But in all there were differences that distinguished every thing and person from the world he knew.

"You haven't told me where we're going," he said.

"Finding our man is one thing," Gan said. "Holding him is another. For that we will need help."

"I'm not sure I'm planning to hold him."

Gan eyed William. "I know, my friend. But I think it is best for you that he be submitted to a hearing."

"You have law enforcement here? I haven't seen anyone who looked like a cop."

"We don't have much in the way of laws. There are constabulary forces, generally rather informal in their organization. With exceptions. The Queen's Guard in Crystalon is one. Cases are generally decided by ad hoc committees assembled as need arises. Judgements are rendered by an assessment of circumstances."

"That works? Sounds pretty loose."

"Well, the entire Labyrinth is in a continual state of change."

"This city seems pretty firmly established."

"Yes, but no place is immune to the shiftings of the Labyrinth. You will understand better after you've been here awhile."

William's attitude hardened. "Just so we're clear, I want a *final* solution."

"Permanent incarceration?"

"If I can be assured of that. Two murdered kids, Gan."

"I do understand, William. If you elect to exact retribution yourself, I will not interfere."

They entered a sprawling, open-air market. The driver let them out and Gan paid him.

They made their way through the crowd, past stalls offering greatly varied merchandise, from clothing to furniture to meats and produce.

Their contact proved to be a rug merchant, a woman whose legs didn't work. She smiled when she saw Gan and rolled to meet them in a wheelchair. She had long, flowing red hair, high cheekbones and arresting blue eyes.

"William, this is Fia Jone," Gan introduced her, "textile merchant extraordinaire, and grand mistress of the occult."

Fia let loose a bright, unrestrained laugh. "And I give you Gan Altum, exalted Poobah of the inflated introduction. Hello, William." She shook William's hand.

"Can we talk in private?" Gan asked.

Fia caught the seriousness in his tone and gestured for them to follow her. She signaled her helper, a young man with Asian features, to take over, and led Gan and William down an aisle between tall stacks of rugs. At the end they went through a door into a work room lined with shelves bearing bottles and vials of unknown substances, and wooden bins containing a great variety of dried plants. The air had a rich, woody odor.

Once they were alone, Gan explained the situation, and William showed Fia the E-fit of Slick.

"Oh, him." She grimaced sourly. "Mean bastard. He's been a problem ever since he crossed. Fancies himself a wizard, which he most definitely is not. He works for Garritch Stormcastle, now."

"You're sure of that?" An edge of trepidation entered Gan's tone inconsistent with his customary bravado.

"Oh, yes. Whatever he's done, it was almost certainly at Stormcastle's behest."

"That means I'm looking for both of them," William said.

Gan and Fia exchanged looks.

"That is beyond you, William," Gan said.

"How so?"

"Stormcastle is a powerful sorcerer. You're no match for him."

William digested the information. "We'll see about that. First I want this guy." He wagged Slick's E-fit.

"We'll need to bind him," Gan told Fia.

"I can help you with that." She wheeled around a work bench to a tall, broad chest with many small, square drawers. She pointed to a drawer near the bottom. "In there."

Gan opened the drawer and lifted out a wooden box engraved with complex, interlacing symbols. He gave it to Fia.

"Who's going to use this?" she asked.

Gan gestured at William.

"Let me have that knife on the table over there."

William fetched the knife. It had a short blade with a sharp point.

"I'm going to need a drop of your blood," she told him. She pricked her own thumb with the knife and squeezed blood on the concentric center of the symbols on the lid of the box. Then she reached for William's hand. He let her prick his thumb with the unsterilized blade, hoping he wasn't exposing himself to infection.

Fia squeezed blood from his thumb as well, stirred the drops together with her forefinger and smeared the blood over the surface of the box.

She held the box up to William. "Say your name, speaking directly to the box."

"William Braden," he said as instructed.

The surface of the box smoked, briefly, and the blood vanished. Fia handed the box to William. "Now you're the only one who can open it."

William frowned at the object uncertainly.

"Go ahead," Fia said, "open it."

He pulled at the lid and it opened, clam-shell style. Inside was a plain, gold bracelet, mounted on a post.

Fia took out the bracelet. "This will prevent him from quickening. It won't otherwise restrain him or make him any less dangerous to deal with physically."

William nodded. "Understood."

"You have to get it on his wrist and close it." She squeezed the bracelet until the ends separated by a gap met. The bracelet underwent a transformation, becoming entirely black and non-reflective, a seamless ring of void. "Once it's closed, only you can remove it."

"Unlikely I'll want to do that."

"Be that as it may, I want you to know how. Take it and tell it to part."

William took the bracelet. It felt cold in his hand. "Part," he said. It returned to its golden state, the gap restored.

"You might want to practice that a few times." Fia looked towards the door, frowning.

"What is it?" Gan asked.

"Shh!" She waved her hand for quiet and wheeled to the door. She sat still a moment, listening. "Get back behind those shelves," she told Gan and William.

Once they were hidden, she opened the door cautiously. Peering between the bottles on a shelf, William saw a tall, black-haired man in a long coat stride purposefully up the aisle toward them. His coat glimmered with elusive colors. The expression in his eyes was dour and determined.

Fia clapped her hands and shouted, "Flurry!" The stacked rugs lining the aisle burst into a chaotic, thrashing tangle, blocking the man's advance. William stared in wonder.

Fia closed the door and locked it. "Out the back, both of you. Return to your ship, Gan, and sail out immediately. Sail Quandary to Minuslitore. He won't think to look for you there."

"But my crew hasn't had time to off-load or load cargo. Quandary!"

"Take your own risks. But if he finds out who you are and catches up to you, I won't be able to help you."

Gan hurried away down a hall adjacent to the shelves. William looked back at Fia. She was making gestures at the closed door and saying things he couldn't understand.

"Come on!" Gan called.

At the end of the hallway they went through a door that opened onto an alley. They ran to the nearest cross street and Gan hailed a rickshaw.

"Harbor," he told the cyclist. As they passed the marketplace, William leaned forward to look toward Fia's stall. A crowd had gathered to watch the rugs fly and whip about.

"Keep out of sight," Gan said sharply, pulling William back under the rickshaw's hood.

"Who was that guy?" William asked.

"Garritch Stormcastle."

Chapter Eleven

Beatrice lived and worked with Mirabel for days she did not count. She learned much of the herbs and their medicinal uses within this new reality she had come to inhabit, and much of the Labyrinth and its denizens, including her teacher. Mirabel had been born in Europe and crossed into the Labyrinth as a child when invaders attacked her country. She had been knocked unconscious when shells hit her home and awakened within the Labyrinth in a place far distant from Keel. A traveling healer had found her, taken her in his care and taught her his calling.

She had never returned to Earth, and now it was a faded, forgotten part of her life lost to the past. She remembered her mother but could not bring the faces of her father or siblings to mind, only the rubble that claimed them. Nor could she remember the city or country of her birth. Of her childhood home she remembered only the kitchen, where she had helped her mother prepare meals.

Mirabel was quite certain that it had been 1916 when she departed her life on Earth. At first Beatrice assumed the old healer's memory deceived her, for that would mean the war she referred to was World War I, and make Mirabel over a hundred years old, still vigorous and spry. But every day Beatrice looked in the mirror and found age receding from her features. Creases with which she was long familiar faded. Clearly some property of the Labyrinth affected the aging process. Beatrice did not hope for a return to youth, but she could not deny that she both felt and looked younger.

One morning she awakened and knew it was time for her to move on. She went into the kitchen and found Mirabel preparing a knapsack for her.

"Where will you go?" the old healer asked, before Beatrice could tell of her intentions.

"I don't know. I imagine I'll take passage on a ship."

"Why would you do that?"

Beatrice had no ready answer.

Mirabel wiped her hands and passed the knapsack to Beatrice. She gave Beatrice's shoulder a pat and said, "Come with me."

Beatrice followed Mirabel up through her garden, as she had, now, many times. When they reached the upper end, Mirabel unlatched a gate there and held it open. She led Beatrice up a dirt path to the cavern wall, and thence into a cave. They had to bow their heads until they reached a dome-like grotto. The grotto was centered by a pool with stone benches around its perimeter. Light from a high opening shone on the pool, where, among lily pads meters broad, a single water lily bloomed, its flower many times larger, and more richly colored, than any Beatrice had ever seen.

Mirabel motioned for Beatrice to sit beside her on a bench.

"You're going to teach me to quicken, aren't you?"

"You don't need to be taught; you've done it. You just need to remember how."

"I don't know where to go."

"You can go where you like."

"I have no place in mind."

"You don't want to go back to the world you know?"

Beatrice thought of the cloister and her sisters, and how pleasant it would be to return to them. But they would not understand what had happened to her, and she had no idea how she might explain. She had never traveled much in the world, but the idea of doing so just to see new sights held no appeal. "I want to learn more of the Labyrinth," she said finally, "but I need to know a place to go to it, don't I?"

"The name is enough."

"You've told me of many places. I don't know how to choose."

"You can also seek a path."

That option resonated deeply with Beatrice. "How do I do that?"

"It may take you into regions of the Labyrinth where you will be entirely alone."

"Well, I can always come back here for company, can't I?"

"You can." Mirabel smiled and patted Beatrice's knee. "You told me you were praying in a chapel when you came here."

"Yes."

"What were you praying for?"

"I don't think I can put it into words. I was trying to go beyond words—outside of them. I don't know if I succeeded."

Mirabel was silent a moment. She gestured at the water lily. "We call that a flower. Hardly adequate, is it?"

"Not adequate at all."

"Words can be flowers too, though, gathered together, like petals in the mind."

"That's a lovely thought. Words have touched me like that many times."

"But for now, a prayer without words."

Beatrice nodded. "Yes."

"That is how you quicken."

Beatrice saw the truth of it.

"Shoulder your bag. I wouldn't want you to leave behind the food I've prepared for you. There's an especially savory pie in there."

Beatrice shouldered the knapsack. "I'd hate to miss that."

"What will you pray for, Beatrice? If you can't put it in words, draw your mind to it however you can."

"Guidance," Beatrice murmured.

"Calm yourself. Become still inside. Gaze upon the flower. I will miss you, Beatrice."

"I will miss you, too, Mirabel."

"Keep looking at the flower, or close your eyes, if you want, and give silent voice to your wordless prayer."

Beatrice made the sign of the cross as she always did before praying, not only in remembrance of Christ's sacrifice, but in acknowledgment of the ever-traveling intersection between the present and the past. She did not close her eyes. She wanted to look at the flower, the way its many colors seeped up from its center and dissolved into white towards the tips of its petals. Without thinking about it she removed her rosary from around her neck and let the beads shift through her fingers, the words she would customarily have spoken translated into sensual expressions of intent that climbed and dove within her body and through its encompassing field in migrating waves.

The flower filled her vision and she fell into its deep, radiant center, the petals closing above her. The heart of the flower became a spiral that dilated at its center, and Beatrice dove through the opening.

The components of a place came into focus, a place unlike any she'd known. Beatrice found herself sitting cross-legged on a flowstone terrace, facing a wild garden vast beyond sight.

"Mirabel?"

Mirabel was not there. She was someplace unknowably distant, and Beatrice was alone again.

In the far reaches before her stood ruins spaced broadly apart. They looked like the ruins of churches and temples: broken domes, gothic arches independent of walls, rows of deteriorating columns absent enclosures. The near cavern wall was lined with titanic sculptures of robed human figures. Sculptures they appeared, and yet they seemed to have accreted via mineral accumulation, or been overcome by it, faces and figures blurred, agleam with seeping wetness.

She felt something climb her arm. Beatrice yanked back her sleeve. Her rosary was winding its way up her forearm, seemingly of its own accord. She pried at the beads, but they pressed more tightly to her skin. She clutched the crucifix in her palm and the rosary chain strained against it.

To her mounting horror, the beads sank into her flesh. Beatrice whimpered in terror. This was nothing she wanted, nothing she'd asked for. She did not want to lose her rosary!

The beads disappeared into her skin, leaving no mark or trace behind. Her rosary, the only link left to her life of devotion, her talisman that had been blessed by Pope John XXIII, was gone. She could not even feel the crucifix against her clenched fingers.

She opened her hand. Where she had clutched the crucifix a tattoo of a stylized water lily appeared in her palm. The manifestation so arrested her that it snuffed anxiety like a douter and her mind stilled.

Beatrice knew that she could not resist what had happened to her, any more than she could understand it. With a wordless prayer she yielded to transformation. An inner wind burst through her, translating her long loneliness into an appreciation of being. Never, never had she felt her faith so deeply confirmed, a faith that neither had nor needed a name, a faith beyond belief.

She staggered down from the flowstone terrace into a meadow of deep grass, and there she collapsed and wept.

Chapter Twelve

When they returned to the *Passenger*, Gan hurried the process of off-loading and taking on cargo, barking commands right and left. William threw himself into helping as he could. Fia had urged them to ship out immediately, but William understood that Gan needed to satisfy his understandings with his crew. He saw Gan argue with Sheply and end it with a slashing gesture.

The *Passenger* left port around midday. William was exhausted, drenched in sweat. He wanted to climb into the water barrel and drink it dry. Grumblings spread among the crew when they saw the direction the ship was taking. William climbed to the aft deck, where Gan stood atop a step platform at the helm.

Gan passed him a pouch of tobacco and some rolling papers. "Sheply picked that up for you. Cigarette tobacco. Probably still stronger than you're used to."

"Much appreciated." William fished out a rolling paper and sprinkled some tobacco in it. The resulting cigarette looked like a misshapen bean pod, but it smoked all right. "Your crew doesn't seem happy."

"We're taking a shorter route to the locks, skipping several ports where we normally trade. The take will be smaller this circuit. On the other hand, they know I'll make the loss up to them out of my own pocket, so they can stow it."

"This because of me? Trying to avoid what's-his-name?"

"I honor my commitments, William. We have no way of knowing what Stormcastle learned from Fia. She is formidable and would not willingly yield information about us or your mission."

"But he might pry it out of her."

"The sooner we get you to Minuslitore, the better."

"That's where you think Slick still is?"

"He favors the brothels there and is not one to resist his appetites. Particularly where women are concerned, unfortunately for the women. It's a good place to start."

Gan steered them into a cavern where the walls met the water on both sides.

"What happened to her legs?"

"Fia?"

"Yeah."

"She lived in a town where the Labyrinth became unstable. She tried to exert her art to stabilize it and got caught in a rock fall."

"This Labyrinth of yours sounds increasingly dangerous, the more I hear about it."

"Have you ever been anyplace that wasn't dangerous?"

William considered. "Maybe not."

"A place is safe until it isn't. Speaking of which, we're sailing through the Sea of Quandary, where the Labyrinth is decidedly less stable. You might want to ride out the trip in my cabin."

William saw that the crew had more than one reason to grumble. Nothing about the waters or the cavern seemed worrisome at the moment. "Well, it looks okay now."

"Hold that thought but keep it to yourself. We sailors are a superstitious lot. We don't like to tempt fate."

They traveled for several days on the Sea of Quandary, never encountering landfall to either side, though in places the cavern broadened so greatly, to and beyond the limits of sight, it was impossible to be certain. Wherever sea met cavern visibly it was as water to wall, without so much as a spur or a sandspit to mitigate the encounter.

William practiced opening and closing the bracelet Fia had given him. It did not have a hinge but proved flexible enough that William was satisfied he wouldn't have trouble getting it on Slick's wrist. The object was disconcerting when closed. He could feel it, solid in his hand, but it had no weight, and however he moved it about it reflected no light. It was in all aspects other than tactile a paradoxical void.

The big cowboy and the levitating fat woman made a rare appearance on the forward deck one afternoon. William positioned himself on a bollard within earshot of them, hoping to overhear their conversation, but they sat together silently, watching the water. He lingered awhile, hoping they might take an interest in him, but they paid him no attention.

He gave up and descended to the main deck. On the way down he glanced back and discovered the fat woman watching him. The look she gave him made him uncomfortable and he hurried away in embarrassment.

That night William was startled awake by a violent rocking of the ship. Gan was not in his bed. William dressed quickly and went outside.

The crew was in a heightened state of activity, battening hatches and reefing the sails. Clouds were massed in the heights above and more darkly in the way ahead. The water was turbulent with high waves. William could see neither land nor cavern wall to port or starboard.

He climbed to the aft deck and found Gan lashed to the helm.

"You have storms in the Labyrinth?"

"Your powers of observation are keen, Detective. Return to my cabin."

William took in the roiling clouds ahead. "I don't think so."

Gan glanced at him. "Then hold onto something. If you're thrown overboard, we won't be able to rescue you."

William positioned himself between two bollards and held tightly to the railing at the forward limit of the aft deck. A lookout scrambled down the shroud from the crow's nest on the foremast, shouting inaudibly and pointing ahead.

The approaching waves were enormously larger, and lightning shone through the oncoming clouds. Lightning that didn't behave like lightning. It didn't flash and vanish; it manifested in vertical columns that lingered and swayed.

Gan spun the wheel, turning the ship to port.

"We can't outrun it!" Sheply shouted.

"I'm not trying to!" Gan shouted back. "Look at the waves! They're running aslant of the keel!"

He straightened his course on a diagonal towards a far cavern wall rendered distantly visible by the approaching lightning. The ship dove into a deep trough and Gan swung it on an arc to starboard, meeting the subsequent wave head on.

He barked an order that Sheply didn't seem to understand. William didn't understand it either. Gan repeated the command. He didn't sound like himself.

William realized Gan wasn't speaking English anymore—he wasn't hearing Gan's speech as English. Sheply, clinging to rigging on the mizzenmast, shouted back. William couldn't understand her either, and it was clear that neither could Gan. Out across the ship, others of the crew were having similar difficulties. Interrupted upon urgent tasks by the realization, some began to panic.

The storm hit in earnest, with horizontal rain that might drown one drawing breath in the face of it. Wind like a barrage of hammers tore open a hatch on the main deck. Water crashed over the gunwales amidships and poured down the open hatch. Gan spun the wheel to cut into a trough that must have been a hundred feet deep, and again arced about to climb the mountainous wave that followed. The sailors were overwhelmed by two kinds of chaos: their inability to communicate and the ferocity of the storm.

Sheply stared about in abject incapacity. William saw that Gan had no attention for anything but steering. The *Passenger* leveled, cresting a swell. William left the security of the railing and strode quickly to Sheply. She couldn't let herself yield to shock. He grabbed her by the shoulders and shook her, pointed from his mouth to his hand several times, and waved at the ship and crew. *Use hand signals, woman; snap out of it.*

She nodded understanding and headed for the stairs. William followed her. A wave bucked the ship to port, and he was nearly thrown overboard. Someone caught him and pulled him back. Sheply.

The ship and crew were cast into more hellish circumstances when the electrical storm surrounded them.

Lightening bore down in swirling columns and drilled the waters like tornadoes of white fire, accompanied by relentless thunder.

For many of the crew it was too much. They huddled in groups, paralyzed by fear, deaf to Sheply's commands and blind to her hand signals. A crack in the clouds opened, like a transient canyon, and William caught a glimpse of the cavern ceiling. Mottled by erratic illumination, it seemed to writhe. They were ants traveling the arteries of a sleeping giant. It didn't have to wake up; if it coughed or rolled over their bones would be home to anemones and urchins or whatever insensate clinging life these weird seas nurtured. The anguished, terrified faces of his crewmates told William the ship was doomed.

But then the archetypes emerged from their cabins. The giant's ten-gallon hat was sucked away by the storm as he stepped on deck. He put his back to the waves crashing over the gunwales and resecured the hatch that had blown open. More incredible was the levitating fat woman. She was not as she had been but clad in armor and a winged helmet like Brunhilda, and she bore a great spear. Neither was she afraid, but possessed of a fierce joy, a titan welcoming contest with the elements. A lightning cyclone veered toward the port side of the ship, and she rode her divan over the gunwales, extending her spear at it. The crackling vortex leapt to the spearhead and the fat woman shrieked with laughter, drawing its force, her body and divan alight with a glow almost too bright to look at. Her helmet blew off and electricity arced from her hair in a blinding penumbra of discharge.

The lightning funnel snaked and writhed above the fat woman but did not break free of her spear. Another cyclone joined it and she held them both, crying out in defiance, behemoth waves crashing about her. The latter vortex bellied toward the ship and grazed the mainmast, setting it afire. The giant climbed the mast and tamped out the flames with his bare hands.

William was so awestruck by these feats that he failed to notice the skinless man. When he did the archetype's actions mystified him. Pellis stood fixed to a place, legs apart, at the center of the main deck. The ship lurched and bucked, and the skinless man leaned and swayed, the positions of his feet never altering. A wave crashed against him and he stood firm.

He met William's gaze. The steadiness in Pellis' eyes was an island of calm in the chaos; they conveyed an appeal and a challenge. William understood as if a voice spoke in his ear: *Know me. Stand with me. Let us be the eye of the storm.*

William recognized in Pellis' calm a state he had experienced himself in times of extreme danger. It was, in fact, part of who he was. When the city had been seized by terror and panic, he had been calm. He had long been one of those who went toward dangers others fled.

He remembered the way the presiding monk in the temple had looked at him, the deep serenity in his eyes. William remembered, too, his defensive tactics training. As a seaman he was useless. He could not help his shipmates save the ship, might get some of them killed if he tried.

But he could be calm.

When people were scared and panicking, the presence in their midst of one composed person could communicate like an antidote.

He made his way to the bottom of the stairs, clinging to the railing. He focused on his center of balance and let go. As the ship pitched and yawed he altered his stance to answer it.

He took one step, and another, until he was an arm's length from Pellis, looking straight in his eyes. They did not speak. They mirrored each other, leaning, bending and straightening at the knees, shifting with the movement of the ship, retaining their positions by force of will. William manifested steadiness beyond his capacity—beyond anyone's. Impossible that waves should crash down and envelop him and he not be swept away; impossible that the ship should toss so violently and he stand rooted to the deck. Something in the connection he shared with Pellis made it possible, and William yielded no attention to wonder about it.

The self-possession in Pellis' eyes was irreconcilable with the grotesquerie, streaming rain in the reeling brightness, of his skinless visage. Skin was the person, what lay beneath subject to scrutiny on the autopsy table or in the medical amphitheater, exposed in life only by wound or surgery. Yet Pellis stood, unwounded, the processes of his body flowing, flexing, sustaining life in plain view. The longer William looked at him, the less horrific he became, the more a person, the more an ally in the exertion of presence. Like discovering a buried truth, William saw Pellis' beauty.

Something changed. William's clothes pulled at him harder in the thrashing wind, as if he'd donned heavier garments without being aware of it. He could only adjust to the encumberment and maintain focus. He heard Sheply order crewmen to go below decks and man the bilge pumps—heard her words as English.

The ship passed beyond the lightning field and the storm relented. William and Pellis continued to stand, facing each other until the seas quieted and William heard English spoken all around him. Then Pellis bowed and William bowed back.

Pellis patted William on the shoulder. "You're one of us, now," he said, and returned to his cabin.

William climbed to the aft deck, where Gan was relinquishing the helm to Sheply. Coming toward William, Gan frowned. "What the hell are you wearing?"

William looked down at himself. His sailor's get-up was gone. He was dressed in grey slacks, a dark jacket, a white shirt and a tie, as he might have worn on the job. But the clothes were not his. His leather boots had been replaced by black, lace-up street shoes with hard soles, and he had on a long, grey trench coat. "I … don't know."

Gan cast a glance sideways, shook his head and sighed. "Oh, hell."

"What?"

Bewildered again, William followed Gan down the stairs as the crew cheered their captain. Halfway down Gan glanced up and stopped. Others followed his gaze and cries of shock and confusion spread across the ship.

Stars. In the ceiling of the cavern was a ragged breach, and the lights of the universe shone through. William recognized constellations he did not know by name, and the vast, luminous river of the Milky Way.

"This isn't possible," Gan said.

"What, you've never seen stars?"

"Never. They are not on the same plane as the Labyrinth."

Pellis came out of his cabin at the bottom of the stairs.

"This is Garritch's doing," Gan said. "That was no natural storm."

"No," Pellis said. "This isn't Stormcastle. This is no human sorcery."

An ache awakened in William's spine and climbed to fill his cranium. He gasped and sank down on the steps, holding his head.

"William?"

The terrible presence that had visited his dream in Keel pressed through William's mind like a diseased shadow. The ache abated and he took long breaths, watching the stars vanish and the cavern ceiling reassert itself. "He's right," he told Gan, "this is something else. Some*one* else." It was like an advance shockwave, precursor to an event far greater. He would have bet money the Hierophant knew what event that would be.

Gan gripped William's arm. "What's going on? What's the matter?"

William struggled for words. "She's coming," he said, not knowing what he meant.

Chapter Thirteen

Beatrice did not know how long she traveled through the caverns of the Labyrinth. She practiced quickening until she became adept at it. When she felt an urge to move on from one place she quickened to another. When she grew hungry, she prayed for food and quickened to a forest or other environ where plant life was abundant. Mirabel had trained her to recognize by smell and sensual instinct what was edible and what was not. Beatrice's body told her what to eat.

She traveled through caverns resplendent with mineral formations—stalactites and stalagmites and grounds covered with flowstone that shimmered with prismatic hues. She traveled through caverns where crystals large as houses grew from the walls. She traveled through caverns where steaming pools scaled down waterfalls hundreds of feet high, and others where waterfalls spilled through voids into nothingness. In most of the places she went, the walls of the caverns shone with their own elusive light, cycling through periods of greater and lesser brightness that mimicked day and night. In a few they did not, illumination issuing weakly from elusive sources Beatrice could not identify. In one of the latter caverns she sensed that she was watched and possibly followed. She did not linger there.

In none of the places she visited did she encounter people. She suspected her yen for solitude was the cause. She was searching for something she could not define. As wondrous and often spectacular as were the sights she encountered, they did not answer the need in her. She had challenged, not for the first time, beliefs she had held since childhood, this time relinquishing them in a quest to confirm their validity.

Despite the confirmation of faith she had experienced, she did not feel that she had validated her beliefs, which was a paradox, and a schism in her being. She missed her rosary, rubbed her arm often, hoping it might resurface. She gave the quandary to God but remained uneasy with the experience.

The faith she had confirmed, the truth she had verified, still she could not put into words, and suspected she might never do. She *had* validated an instinct she'd had, that what people in the world she'd known through the majority of her life were pleased to call truths were in fact shadows of things much vaster and more elusive than were generally supposed, beyond even the reaches of the universe. Even that universe, as incomprehensibly vast as it was, did not comprise the whole of existence. It was but a facet of something greater.

But what of the beliefs that had defined her life? Had she given her years and decades, her youth and all of her ages, to falsehoods and fiction? She could hear a chorus of skeptics smugly trumpet assent. She was awakening, they would say, to the real truth: that life was purposeless, the soul and even the person a fiction, and God a bedtime story lent canonical imprimatur. Christ was merely a tragic figure whose sad crucifixion at best represented a failed protest for social justice. He had not represented any aspect of God, nor substantiated any metaphysical design.

Through much of her life her mind had spilled and churned with the texts of countless books, each tasking or complementing the others. Somehow her faith had survived those contests, much though she had often wondered if it mattered what face one put on God. The thought of studying further made her tired. She was not looking for an answer in the past; she was looking for herself in the present.

She had divested herself of the trappings of sisterhood, left them folded on a bed in the room she had shared with William. Familiar as those trappings had been, and in spite of the affection she held for them, she did not miss them. They had been her declaration to the world that she had left worldly ways behind, along with the hungers they inspired. They were armor she no longer needed.

Now, though she still walked barefoot, she wore a simple, brown dress that was loose and comfortable, and let her hair fall free. She looked down at her feet, firm upon the wild, mysterious ground, supporting her, body, mind and spirit, in her search.

She noticed that, in this cavern again, there were ruins in the wilds she passed through. As in the first cavern she'd quickened to from Keel, the ruins appeared to be the remains of churches and temples of various faiths.

She stopped and peered at the far cavern walls, spotted the row of giant statues, and realized she had returned to that cavern.

She entered a ruin that appeared Christian in origin, its roofless walls, where intact, perforated by gothic windows long paneless. Flying buttresses supported the remnant walls from without.

In the center of the sanctuary she encountered a pool surrounded, at regular intervals around its perimeter, by statues of human figures in long robes. As with the titanic figures lining the cavern's wall, time, weather and mineral accretion had blurred their features, erasing all identifying aspects.

The waters were clear and purled gently; lush vegetation grew to their verge. Wisps of steam rose from the pool's surface. Underwater plants lolled in its depths, and small, colorful fish darted about. Beatrice took off her dress and stepped into the pool, relishing the warmth and ease that enveloped her body. She found a comfortable place to sit, and there, immersed to her chin, she closed her eyes and invited God to inhabit her with His voice, should it be Her will to do so. She listened for God's voice not in her mind but her senses, opening herself without limitation or expectation to whatever might come.

Her memories coursed like rivers, the faces and facts of her history translated into sensual streams. The range of human feelings was not limited by, and was much more varied than, the words catalogued to name them—yet again she had that perception. Belief, too, was translated into a sensual experience, reaffirming the wonder of existence. Such blooms, such mysteries rose in her, far greater than certainties, greater than names. From their center a voice composed of all that she was and all that she felt, composed of taste, inner vision, sensation, smell, sound and emotion, spoke in an ineffable language a response that could only inadequately be translated as, *"You are."*

Beatrice opened her eyes, sat up and looked down at the water. The ripples cleared and she saw herself reflected as she had been as a young woman, all the creases and weathering of old age erased. She smiled, somewhat wistfully, until a tiny red fish kissed the surface of the water in the center of her reflected forehead, and Beatrice realized that she was seeing herself as she now was.

She averted her gaze. Nothing in this place was comprehensible. Desires she'd laid to rest roused with disturbing suddenness. Beatrice took long breaths, calming herself. It was one thing to regain a measure of vigor and have a few furrows recede, another to return headlong to a state fifty or more years removed.

Her hands were smooth, the distended veins on their backs, the gauze of creases in her palms, all gone. She felt her face. Its texture agreed with the reflection, free of roughness or wrinkle.

Young.

Beatrice scrambled from the pool and sat on the bank hugging her knees. First her rosary and now this—these transformations were not incidental. There was direction in them, an arcane logic. Something was being asked of her.

She closed her eyes and focused again on her breathing. She knew the maelstrom of fear; its makeup was always the same, differing only in its composition. She was in the wrong place, subject to the wrong influences, unequal to unknowable challenges, prey to blind forces and deceptive designs. Time, time, time was running out.

The meat of elliptical reasoning and panic.

Beatrice breathed.

So preoccupied had she been with beliefs that she had strayed from seeking her purpose. That objective did not require travel; she could serve it in stillness. Whatever agencies moved time and space ever manifested change—daily, hourly, throughout life, wherever one was. Beatrice had too much compared her experiences in the Labyrinth with those of her life on Earth, looking back and back to calibrate their distinctions. She sat quietly, breathed, and let herself be where and when and as she was.

Some unmeasurable period later she rose and put her dress back on. She wanted to look at her reflection again but resisted the urge. That was exactly the sort of desire that restored, when resisted, self-possession to the being. She stood still amid the quiet plants and mineral-encrusted statues, made the sign of the cross and prayed, again, for guidance.

She opened her eyes to find herself seated on a chair-like stalagmite at a table-like flowstone pedestal, facing an immense wall of doors. The wall rose hundreds of feet and spanned a cavern many times as broad, the doors that comprised it innumerable. The doors were all of the same dimensions, but each, in other aspects, unique—some wooden, some metal, some painted, some plain, some in differing ways ornate. Most showed signs of long weathering.

Upon the pedestal rested a deck of cards, just forward of which an inscription in the surface of the pedestal read:

Know Your Path

Shuffle, Cut, and Turn the Top Card

Beatrice grimaced sourly. She'd shunned the association but now she really did feel like Alice. She wouldn't have been surprised to encounter next a hookah-smoking caterpillar.

The relationship between self-determination and chance was one of the great puzzles. To apply to an oracle went against Beatrice's grain. Then again, the circumstances of birth could be viewed as God dealing the soul a hand. Unless the soul, beyond the veil of birth, dealt one to itself.

Beatrice sighed and did as the inscription instructed.

The card she turned over bore an artful rendering of a three-sided pyramid, viewed from directly above its apex. At each of its three base points were spoked wheels, such as might serve for the helms of ships.

Beatrice found the imagery comforting, not knowing if her reflexive interpretation of its symbolism were in any way accurate.

Mechanical noise drew her attention. With a great clamor of rattling and clanging, the doors shifted about in a manner too complex to track. Eventually a door slid into place before her and opened. Three other doors immediately above it took on a bluish glow.

Beatrice rose and approached the open door. She could see nothing through its frame but a silken blackness.

She stopped at the threshold. She did not know what she risked by crossing it. Nor could she imagine a more straightforward response to her prayer.

An inner voice she trusted coaxed her to go ahead. She stepped through the doorway.

With all she had thus far encountered in the Labyrinth, Beatrice had come to expect surprise from each new place she visited. But the sights that met her this time so amazed her that it was some while before she could do more than gape and stare.

The place might once have been a cavern, but in its current disposition was more like a titanic hall. The walls had been cut into overlapping rectangular shapes, like giant fused blocks, similar to what one might encounter in a quarry. But there had never been a quarry like this, that extended to unseeable distances in both directions.

Far more astonishing than the geometry of the hall, though, were the vast murals painted on its walls. To her right, giant human figures, all nude, were captured in an ecstatic celestial dance through a firmament strewn with galaxies and nebulae. To her left, amid radiating color fields, stood the figure of a man, perhaps a hundred feet tall, assembled out of the elemental stuff of abstraction. His hair was short and neatly combed and he had a Van Dyck beard. Clad in a tweed three-piece suit, he held his right hand extended, palm up, above which hovered a flower like an iris.

The floor was paved in glazed tiles of many shapes and colors that formed interlacing geometric patterns into the distances. The ceiling was yet another inexplicable wonder. In defiance of gravity, a luminous, blue river traveled its channel.

Beatrice drifted down the hall in a rapt state of awe, viewing giant landscapes, cityscapes, figurative works, surrealist fantasies, abstractions, all of breathtaking magnificence. She wished William were with her to share these wonders.

She stopped, caught by the emptiness of the hall. Surely the inhabitants of the Labyrinth must visit this place, but she was still alone. She did not know if her initial inclination to solitude still exerted influence, but here she was, alone again. She'd had enough of solitude. She was over-ready to be among people.

She heard a soft scuffing sound, peered ahead and saw that she was wrong. There was someone else present. Beatrice suppressed the urge to run and strode toward the person at a casual gait.

His vestments surprised her, when she drew near enough to make them out. The man was dressed like a bishop. He was viewing some work recessed from her view. Drawing closer, she began to doubt her impression of his office. The symbols on his robe were alien to her. His mitre, too, was odd in its colors and adornments. His staff bore a triumvirate cross at its apex—perhaps he was affiliated with some Eastern Orthodox faith.

Past the edge of a mural depicting a ship caught in a terrible storm, Beatrice saw scaffolding. The work the tall man viewed she discovered to be yet in progress, its painter high upon a raised platform.

Becoming cognizant of the nature of the work she was taken aback. It described a whirling maelstrom of dismembered human limbs and body parts, faces torn, ruptured and whole in anguish amid geometric abstractions indecipherably complex.

"What on Earth is he painting?" she gasped.

The oddly dressed man glanced at her. "Nothing on Earth," he said, returning his attention to the mural. "Not yet."

"I should hope not." Beatrice frowned at him. "Yet?'"

"It is interesting, is it not," he said, after an extended silence, "that the pattern is recursive."

Beatrice marshaled her emotions and examined the painting as dispassionately as she could. "I see what you mean. It's a fractal, isn't it." A fractal of hell. She peered up at the artist. He was painting with his eyes closed. "He's not looking at what he's doing."

"He is blind," the tall man said. "He has been working on this painting," he paused in contemplation, "for a very long time."

"Are you a priest?"

The man shook his head faintly. "My vestments are as the Labyrinth provides. They have changed over the millennia."

"*Millennia?* You're as old as *that?*"

"Age and time no longer concern me."

The man turned his gaze to meet hers. Beatrice saw in his eyes a depth of power and knowledge that made her shudder. "Mirabel told me of ones like you. You're an archetype, aren't you?"

"No. I am something else. Some regard me as a guardian, though that is inaccurate as well. My name is Cabal. I am Hierophant to the Labyrinth of Souls. I conduct passage for those who seek to enter the school of the Labyrinth by the ways of coins, staves, blades or cups." He studied Beatrice. "You did not enter by any of those ways."

"I … entered by the way of prayer."

The Hierophant continued his scrutiny, making some assessment. "No. You think that, I have no doubt. You are not given to dishonesty. But you are mistaken."

Beatrice stiffened. "By what way then did I enter?"

"By the way of unknowing. Very few enter that way. It requires that one relinquish both self and certainty, which few possess the mettle to do. I know this because it was my way as well, though I think I was slower and more stubborn than you."

"I did not come here on purpose."

"In that we differ."

"You knew of this place?"

"I learned of the Labyrinth in ancient texts."

"I know of no texts that teach of a place like this."

"On the planet they have been lost. Destroyed, forgotten or disavowed to molder in humanity's amnesia. The knowledge echoes, there, in the writings of authors of many disciplines, even fiction, as it cannot help but do, this place being ineluctably human. The accurate texts, though, are gone from the upper world. I read them and became obsessed with entering this reality. I was nearly dead from old age, like yourself, before I succeeded."

"How do you know that? How do you know anything about me?"

"I know little specifically. I have been waiting for you. You are the fourth."

"Fourth what? I don't understand that."

"You are needed. The cards have shown it. Four are needed, and you are the fourth. I yielded our need to the will of the Labyrinth, and it has led us to each other."

Beatrice felt the truth of Cabal's words collapse through her like an inescapable calamity. "Needed for what?" she made herself ask.

"To answer a terrible travail lest it consume us all." Cabal gestured at the blind artist's mural. "Behold the void at its center. *She* comes for us."

Beatrice looked at the center of the mural, where an irregularly circular space was given to purest black. It seemed to reach out for her, a shock of nothingness, a tentacled obesity of despair, a void so deep all the faith in the universe couldn't fill it. Beatrice vomited, stricken by a terror that lanced the core of her being. The blind artist had rendered something horrific beyond words. The blackness swirled invisibly and was inhabited by a will.

Chapter Fourteen

The day after the storm the lookout on the mainmast shouted down, pointing to an object flying towards them through the heights behind the ship. It proved to be the giant cowboy's ten-gallon hat. A crewman caught it, knocked on the giant's door and delivered it to him.

A short while later a second hat made entrance, this one landing securely on William's head. William took it off and appraised it, understanding it to be part of his new, involuntary costume. A dark grey fedora with a black band. He sighed, missing his beloved porkpie hat, which had vanished during the storm. Permanently, it seemed.

William was amazed that no crew had been lost, and the ship not suffered greater damage than it had. He didn't talk to Gan about the worry that possessed him. William could not reconcile his growing sense of an unknown danger with his determination to punish Slick.

Neither could he keep from thinking about it. To dismiss that things beyond his comprehension underlie his circumstances would have been bald-faced self-deception.

Slick had told him that he hadn't known what he was into. Chasing him, William had been thrown increasingly into bizarre situations beyond his experience. He didn't know why the Hierophant had cast him into the Labyrinth, and he didn't know Slick's motive for killing the Crenshaws.

He tried to examine the matter as he would the elements of a case. The obvious implication was that Slick's motives and Cabal's were somehow related. Related but not the same. William couldn't ignore the possibility that the dovetail between them was the indefinable danger he now sensed. Which raised the question of whether he should continue looking for Slick or try to figure out what else was going on.

The killings could have been incidental to another purpose. The idea that they had been some kind of experiment had been raised by both McCleary and Yoshi. Maybe the experiment had been not to test the black stuff, but to learn or verify something else.

None of his questions were answerable without further information. If he were going to change course, he needed a course to change to. As the days aboard the *Passenger* wore on, William became increasingly frustrated.

One morning he awakened to the sound of rushing water. He went on deck. The mouths of two other caverns yawned, right and left, their seas joining with Quandary's.

The surface of the water was calm, nearly smooth, though it seemed to be moving swiftly. William noted that the sails had been raised. He climbed to the foredeck. The sound of rushing water grew louder. In the distance ahead there seemed a perimeter, arcing into mist-enshrouded distances to either side, beyond which the mingled seas vanished.

William grabbed a crewman going by. "Are we approaching a waterfall?"

The sailor smiled and nodded. "We're almost to Minuslitore."

William held onto him. "But the waterfall, that isn't a problem?"

The sailor laughed and pointed. "We go down through the locks."

William noticed several structures, like watchtowers on the battlements of a castle, situated along the perimeter of the approaching falls. One stood directly ahead, ships lined up in front of the *Passenger* moving towards it. William made out a ship emerging from the nearest of the structures to port, and another row of ships lined up on approach to the nearest one to starboard.

The ship ahead of them passed through a gate into a stone channel and the gate closed. A tugboat came alongside the *Passenger*, and crewmen threw down lines. The tugboat positioned itself behind the ship and slowed its advance. The gate opened and the tugboat released the lines. The *Passenger* went through the gate and entered a channel between stone walls high as the main deck. Lines were thrown to crews atop the walls. They tied the lines to cleats welded to chains that traveled gutters running the lengths of the walls, thus controlling the advance of the ship.

The archetypes were on the foredeck. William approached them. He no longer had a reason not to. Whatever changed them had changed him, too.

"Been meaning to thank you all for saving the ship." He had to shout to make himself heard over the noise of the falls.

"Everyone saved it," the giant said. "You too." He extended his hand, which engulfed William's. "Bill Grundy."

"William Braden."

The levitating fat woman introduced herself as Crisis. She reached in a pocket in her divan and handed William a card. In gold letters embossed on a red background, it read:

Le Cabaret des Archétypes

William gave her a questioning look.

"It's our club. You're a member, now. Easiest place to quicken to; just think the name and wish it. Come by and we'll buy you a round."

"First timers drink for free, Crisis," Pellis said.

"So, he'll be a cheap date. Picked out a name for yourself?" she asked William.

"What's wrong with the one I've got?"

"You're an archetype, now. You need a name." She appraised him. "He looks like Humphrey Bogart. How about 'Bogie?' You like that?"

"Not much."

Crisis laughed. "Right. Bogie it is."

William wasn't going to argue with a woman who jousted with lightning tornadoes.

Around midday, the *Passenger* entered the uppermost lock, and William had his first view of the falls. He'd never had a problem with heights, but he had a brief pass with vertigo, and clung to the gunwale. A wall of water plummeted from an endless precipice that might have been the edge of the world. The drop was at least a thousand feet. Tiny in the distance below, upon a far shore, a city spread among a thicket of curious vertical structures that spanned the cavern floor to ceiling.

Through the windows of a wheelhouse on the forward right corner of the lock, William watched several stout men turn a massive horizontal wheel, pushing on spokes that radiated from it. A mammoth chain composed of links bigger than William was rode up a vertical gutter in the wall under the wheelhouse. The ship sank into a stone well until the view was lost. The thunder of the falls became a muted drone.

The sound reached deep places in William. He watched Bill Grundy sit on a bollard, tilt his head back and close his eyes. William closed his own eyes and listened. It reminded him of the chanting of the monks but went deeper. Chant of water; chant of the world.

Eventually the ship stopped sinking. William looked up at the wet stone walls that now reached high above them. He guessed they'd descended at least a hundred feet. A gate opened, lines were thrown forward, and they were guided into the second lock.

Now the falls showered about them, and the roar made speech impossible. Each lock had its own crew and wheelhouse. William wondered what state it put a man in, to spend his days in the constant presence of such a profound music. He stood at the gunwale, reveling in the spray on his face. It brought out the smells of the ship: the resin in the decking, the rope of the shrouds. He saw Sheply, across the ship on the aft deck, shout in Gan's ear to make herself heard.

Twelve locks they descended through, each a hundred feet or more deep. And each time they emerged from the well of a lock, the spectacle of the falls embraced them from a new perspective, always with incomparable grandeur.

When finally they exited the bottom lock, everyone was in an altered state. Even there, thousands of feet from the base of the falls, the water roiled from the tumult of falling water. William gazed back at the locks with admiration. Supported to their heights by gargantuan flying buttresses, they had to be one of the greatest engineering feats of humanity, and people on the planet of his birth knew nothing of them.

William crossed the ship to the aft deck.

Gan nodded at him from the helm, understanding in his eyes. "Impressive, isn't it?"

"There aren't words," William said. "Do they have a name?"

"The Falls of Isis."

"The Egyptian god?"

"Goddess. Most powerful of them all."

William gazed at the soaring curtain of water and found the name fitting.

Gan steered toward the city William had seen from the heights. A multitude of pillars, spanning the cavern floor to ceiling, clustered in and about the city. William could not discern their nature, but he did not ask Gan about them. Taken by the spirit of adventure, he wanted to discover them for himself.

And so it was that they came to the great port city of Minuslitore.

Chapter Fifteen

The approach to the city wound among giant mineral columns that extended from the water's depths all the way to the cavern's ceiling, products of stalactites and stalagmites joining untold ages ago, before the sea commanded its current bed. The columns, bedizened with flowstone draperies, had been translated into habitats, encircled by windows, balconies and terraces. They were taller than any skyscraper in New York—Gan estimated two or three thousand feet in height. Small boats and flying crafts circulated among them.

Even as they entered the harbor, with the chatter and hum of the city loudening, the sound of the Falls retained a susurrant presence. There were more steam ships in Minuslitore's harbor, but sailing vessels still dominated.

The city inhabited its environment with such grace it seemed to belong there by natural right. The immense columns were more numerous on land, connected by countless bridges. Buildings excavated from other mineral formations or constructed of stone, none more than a few storeys tall, lined meandering streets. The roadways were crowded with pedestrians and vehicles of many kinds, the compliment of flying crafts, predominately helicopters and dirigibles, much greater than in High Harbor.

William bid the archetypes and his shipmates farewell. He clasped Sheply's hand and drew her close. "Thanks for saving my life."

She chucked him on the chin and walked away. He watched her until she looked back. He tipped his hat and she smiled.

Gan accompanied William off the ship and led him to a transit platform, where they boarded a dirigible with several other people. As they rose into the air William saw that there were also canals through the city that small boats traveled. There were large mineral pools, too, some of which steamed, and were obviously popular with bathers.

"Where are we going?" he asked Gan.

"Brothel district, near the town center."

William watched dirigibles pass like flying whales among the columns, and veritable swarms of helicopters, most with single, unenclosed seats. He noticed that small landing pads studded the columns at intervals up their flanks, saw helicopters land on and depart from them. The streets bustled with activity below. On balconies that protruded from the giant columns and nestled in their flowstone crannies, denizens hung laundry, read, mingled, took their ease.

The dirigible sank towards an open-air plaza centered by a park, where brightly colored flowers massed concentric gardens. The smell of the blooms wafted up like a greeting. From the platform they traveled on foot into environs beshadowed by a closeness of columns. They passed into streets lined by bars and nightclubs, some clearly involved in sex trade. The air grew less pleasant, threaded with odors of refuse and rot. William regarded evidence of the coarser aspects of human dispassion philosophically. Here as everywhere, lonely, dissatisfied people sought release.

Gan led William toward a column encircled at street level by many entrances. They stopped at a black door flanked by lantern sconces that glowed red. The sign above the door was in a language William could not read, words in strange script centered by a stylized rendering of a naked woman standing with her legs apart and her arms spread upwards.

They entered a dim, low-ceilinged establishment illumined only by candlelight. William took in black walls and red leather booths, round-topped tables, loosely arranged sofas and armchairs, a dozen or so patrons kept company by scantily clad women and lithe young men.

A lean woman in a dark pants suit approached them, smiling. "Gan! Here's a rare delight. It's been ages." She wore her short, grey-streaked black hair combed back and smoked a cigarette in a long red holder. She stroked Gan's face affectionately.

"William, this is Mercy, mistress of this establishment."

"Welcome to The X Club, William. Any friend of Gan Altum's is gladly received. Where have you been, Gan? I've missed you. I'd begun to think you'd forgotten us."

"That would never be possible, Mercy." Gan glanced around uneasily. "There's a woman in Pinchwood who cares about me."

Mercy looked down at Gan with mock disapproval. "Making an honest man of you?"

"Alas, I fear she is."

Mercy's expression softened. "You poor thing."

"We'd like to talk with you privately," Gan said

Mercy gave William an appraising look. She signaled them to follow her and led them to a half-circle booth in an enclosed nook at the end of the bar. Mercy shooed away young women lounging there.

The three sat down. Gan nodded at William. William showed Mercy the E-fit of Slick.

Her expression darkened. "The nasty one. What's he done?"

"It might be better if you don't know," William said.

Mercy gave him back the E-fit. "He pays extra for pain."

William didn't like the glibness with which Mercy delivered this report. "To receive or inflict it?"

"Both." The madam quailed at the heat in William's scrutiny. "No one forces anyone to do anything. Some girls like it. We make it clear that stop means stop."

William studied Mercy's expression. "I'm sensing a 'but' dangling there."

She swallowed. "We've had to expel him a couple of times."

"And yet you let him back in."

"With sternly expressed understandings. He pays very well."

"When did you last see him?" Gan asked.

Mercy's eyes darted about, scanning the club.

William knew that look. "He's here, isn't he?"

She gave a surreptitious nod.

"Where?" William leaned toward her.

Mercy stiffened. "What do you want him for? Tell me."

"Murdering a family, including the kids."

She stared at William in horror. "That's nothing to do with me!"

"Where?" William pressed.

The madam took another careful look around, then whispered, "Room seven, second floor." She masked gesturing at the entry to a steep flight of stairs with re-lighting her cigarette.

William scooted out of the booth and strode toward the stairs. Gan followed but William stopped him. "You don't want to be part of this."

"I do."

William looked hard at Gan. "Your choice." He headed up the stairs.

One flight up, a curving green corridor extended right and left. Gan pointed right. At the end of the hall, William found room seven on the right. He put his ear to the door and heard voices, male and female. That and whipping sounds.

"You like that?" Whap! "No, and you're not meant to." Whap!

"Fuck you!" Whap! "Sick motherfucker!" Whap!

William turned the knob quietly. Through a slender opening he saw Slick and a young woman, both naked, trade blows with elongated leather paddles.

William gave the door a push and let it swing open.

Slick whirled on him. "Hey, fuck-dick, occupied!" He froze when he saw William's gun.

William signaled the young woman to leave. She snatched up her clothes and slipped by him.

Slick straightened, taking a breath. "Do I know you?"

William stepped into the light and pushed his hat back with his thumb. "Did you know Wendy Crenshaw?"

Slick frowned. His eyes widened and his lips twisted into a wicked grin.

"That's right, asshole."

"Well, I'll be fucked. The arm of the NYPD is definitely getting longer."

"Long enough. Get dressed."

Slick sauntered to the chair where his clothes hung.

William beat him to it, extracted the 9mm Glock from the shoulder holster concealed by Slick's leather flight jacket and pocketed it. "People keep giving me guns."

Slick smirked and pulled on his clothes. He leaned on the chair, bending for his shoes, and William slapped the bracelet on his wrist.

Slick frowned at the bracelet, grinned again. "Ain't you the clever one."

Gan tossed Slick's shoes across the room. "He'll be easier to manage barefoot."

That earned Gan a dark look. "Gonna remember this, midget."

"I truly hope so," Gan replied.

Slick pulled on his jacket and returned his attention to William. "So, now what?"

William stroked the trigger with his forefinger. He had never killed a defenseless man.

"If you're gonna shoot me, get it over with."

"There's law enforcement?" William asked Gan.

"I can have Mercy summon them. I don't know what their response will be. Can you give evidence of his acts?"

Slick's grin broadened. He knew William couldn't prove anything.

"Find me something to tie his hands with," William told Gan. "I don't have my cuffs."

Gan looked around, pulled a sheet from the bed and tore strips from it.

"That'll do," William said. "Turn around." He shook his gun at Slick.

Slick never surrendered his crappy grin. William knew his mind was working. "Try something. Give me a reason."

Slick turned and put his hands back. Gan looped the linen strips around his wrists.

"Tie them tight," William said.

"I'm gonna remember this, too." Slick said.

Gan yanked the bonds tighter. "Maybe if I hunt around I can find the shit I give. Hold still."

Slick bucked backwards, sending Gan reeling into William. William shoved Gan aside, but Slick was out the door. The squirrely son-of-a-bitch was fast.

William tore after him. He didn't want to risk a shot in the hallway. Slick made it to the stairs and leapt up them.

William pursued. Two flights up he found the linen strips on the steps, two more and he stopped. He didn't see Slick or hear him.

Something creaked above him. He continued up quietly and heard footsteps again, running higher. Goddam, the bastard was fast.

William lost count of how many flights he climbed. His thighs burned from the strain.

He stopped again. The footsteps weren't above him, they were receding down the hall on the floor he'd just passed. He jumped back to the landing in time to see Slick go through a door at the end of the passage, about a hundred feet away, and cut right. Following, William found himself on a portico that joined series of balconies, right and left.

He heard commotion to the right, jumped over a balustrade and dodged getting clocked by an angry woman with a bat. He jumped the next balustrade, the woman cursing behind him. Chairs, potted plants, a table and laundry had been tossed to impede his pursuit. Past several more balconies defiled by Slick's vandalisms William arrived at another portico. People lounging on deck chairs, already disconcerted, gave him wary looks. They saw his gun and fled inside.

"Which way did he go?" William called after them.

He holstered the gun. Three bridges extended from the portico to adjacent columns. William ran from one to the next, peering across to the far columns. "God *damn* it!"

To William's amazement, Gan rose up near him flying an unenclosed, single-seat helicopter. From the way it wobbled he didn't seem to have great control of the thing.

"The middle bridge!" he shouted. "The middle one!" The helicopter veered off in a wide arc, Gan wrestling with the steering handle.

William ran for the middle bridge. A diagonally striped bar had lowered across the entrance. A blaring noise like a foghorn drew his attention right. A giant dirigible rounded into view, negotiating its way between the columns. The bridge to the right had parted in its center, the halves rising to make way for the blimp. The bridge he wanted to cross was parting too.

"Fuck it." William ducked under the barricade and sprinted up the rising drawbridge. He leapt across the gap. The edge of the far span hit him in the chest. He barely managed to pull himself over. The dirigible blew its horn again. William caught a glimpse of the pilot gaping at him. He lost his footing on the steepening bridge span, slipped and tumbled down, his back slamming against the barrier at the bottom. He rolled under it, moaning, dragged himself to his feet, pain stabbing him front and back.

He leaned against the balustrade, hugging his chest, saw people tiny in the street below. "You're out of your mind, Braden."

He staggered through a doorway into a hall where several confused-looking people stood.

"Did an asshole run through here?"

A tall, stout man with a braided goatee pointed at a stairwell.

William made himself run, took the stairs three at a time, wincing as he went. He made it to the ground floor, dodged through an indoor market, stopped on the landing outside and scanned the crowd in a plaza. He spotted Slick, weaving through the crowd at a swift stride, about three hundred feet away. Not running, blending in.

William leapt down the steps, couldn't see Slick through the crowd. He jumped up, searching for him, thought he'd lost him, then spotted Slick ducking left into a three-story stone building. William forced himself to speed up, his chest aching like fire, stumbled into pedestrians as he went, got cursed and yelled at some more.

He made it to the door Slick had gone through. Inside was a large lobby, at the far end of which a short flight of red-carpeted steps led to a hallway. William hurried through, scanning people lounging in armchairs. He didn't see Slick. He climbed the stairs, stopped briefly at the top to catch his breath.

The hall was empty. William jogged down it, came to a crossing hallway.

On instinct he turned left to find his way blocked by Cabal.

The Hierophant's expression was unyielding. He would not let William pass.

"Jesus fuck me." William sought heavenward, threw his hands up and let them drop. "Why should I be surprised to see you?"

Chapter Sixteen

William rode with Cabal up through the heights among the giant mineral columns in a helicopter that, from its hissing expulsions of vapor, seemed to be steam powered. The cavern was deep in dusk, near nightfall. William looked down at the city, now teeming with lights. Gan would be searching for him. William hoped he would have a chance to explain, sometime. The grim set of Cabal's face told him all he needed to know about that time not being now.

The inscrutable son-of-a-bitch had assured him that everything would be made clear. This had better be good.

"Any of these towers have elevators?"

"Some," Cabal said.

William waited for more. "Not a scintillating conversationalist, are you?"

Near the ceiling of the cavern, the pilot landed on a pad that extended from a column a short distance from its crown. William followed Cabal up a stairway to the top storey. At the end of a short, red-carpeted corridor, Cabal opened a door.

William felt like he'd walked into the penthouse of an upscale Manhattan apartment building. A large living room with plush beige carpeting spread before him, pale-green, armless sofas and rust-colored armchairs invitingly arrayed amid pole lamps, built-in dark wood cabinets and low oval tables. At the far end of the room a vertically slatted wood partition isolated what, through the slats, looked to be an office.

"Wait," Cabal told William. He crossed the room and went down a hall.

Plate glass spanned the left side of the room. William gazed out at the city. The roof of the cavern, crowded with stalactites, looked almost near enough to touch from the long balcony outside. The falls were a pale blue band in the distance. Lights shone in windows up and down the columns. His frustrations notwithstanding, William felt privileged to have this view.

He heard steps behind him. A strikingly beautiful woman emerged from the hallway. She wore a long, white, belted robe. Auburn hair swept back from her sensuous face in a natural, wavy fall.

She came directly to William, extending her hand. "Detective Braden, thank you for joining us." Her voice had a musical lilt and was arrestingly clear.

"I'm not sure I had a choice." He shook her hand. Warmth and goodness emanated from the woman. Tension eased in William's shoulders. He recognized that she was one of those rare, genuine beings whose mere presence made one feel better.

"I am Lark Niamh Ó Cadhla, Guardian of the Traveling Doors and High Steward of Minuslitore."

William didn't know how to respond. "I don't want to be rude, but I would appreciate it if someone explained why I'm here."

"You are not rude at all. The simplest answer is that the Labyrinth has led us to each other. That is not quite accurate, for it suggests predestination, which is not a factor."

"I did not mean that to be an existential question."

"It is better to let some understandings come to you than to seek them," Lark said, "much as that may run counter to the investigative instincts of a detective."

"Those instincts are hard-earned. They've served me well."

"And I have no doubt that they will continue to serve you, only not so well in this regard. This asks a different discipline, in which attention is primary and inquiry plays a lesser role. I think you are not entirely unfamiliar with that discipline."

William, unsatisfied, twisted his lips skeptically.

"I do not mean to be evasive," Lark said. "It will be easier to clarify our circumstances, to the extent that they can be, with everyone present. Let me assure you, though, that I in no way condone the wicked acts of the person you pursued here. For myself, I think you would be justified in killing him. I doubt it would trouble me to kill him myself. I ask, however, that you forebear. There is a much more dire concern that requires our attention."

"You need him for something so don't kill him."

"Not exactly, but in essence, yes."

"What's the other thing?"

"Preventing the destruction of Earth and its Labyrinth."

William thought she was joking. She wasn't. There wasn't a hint of sarcasm in her tone nor insincerity in her eyes.

●

Beatrice answered the knock at her door. Cabal stood in the hallway, his somber demeanor unreadable as ever.

"We are gathering." He extended his hand toward the living room.

Beatrice stepped out and preceded him down the hall. Hearing William's voice she stopped. "Is this why I became an archetype?" she heard him ask.

"The designs of the Labyrinth are never so singular," Lark answered. "You have always been part of something greater than yourself. That has become more evident …"

Beatrice backed down the hall. "You did not tell me William Braden was here," she said in a hushed voice. The Hierophant was good at masking his reactions, but Beatrice marked his surprise. He had not known that William and she were acquainted. "What he said—he's an archetype?"

"He has undergone that transformation, yes."

"Have I?"

"No."

"You're sure of that?"

"I am."

"But William is here for the same reason as I?"

Cabal studied her a moment before answering. "He is the third, yes."

Beatrice closed her eyes and brought her fist to her mouth.

"I am curious—"

"I'd appreciate it if you wouldn't speak for a moment." Beatrice strove to assert inner calm. All the hells and heartaches born of yearning, and what was life worth without them? "What is happening to me, Cabal? You know things. Tell me."

"You are undergoing a change; its exact nature I do not know. One could say that you are being prepared for an ordeal, and that might be true. One could say that you are preparing yourself, and that might be equally true, or truer."

He said nothing further. Beatrice didn't know how to frame a question that might pry a less opaque answer from him. "If William doesn't recognize me, don't tell him who I am." She smoothed the sides of the khaki jump suit Lark had provided her, raised her chin and proceeded to the living room.

It was plain that William had undergone a profound change, though the steadiness in his eyes, the clarity of purpose in his bearing, remained. A frown creased his brow, but he did not recognize her. Lark noticed her and started to introduce them. Beatrice signaled her not to with a surreptitious head shake and was relieved when understanding flashed in Lark's eyes.

William sensed something unspoken in the unaccountably awkward silence. The tall young woman who had entered with Cabal seemed familiar. She possessed the quality Lark had, the fiber and warmth that put one at ease. With these two women in the room the Labyrinth was a much more agreeable place. Any place would be. Beatrice would like them, he thought, and hoped she was all right.

The unknown woman stayed near the hallway and it seemed no one would introduce them. William glanced from Lark to Cabal. No quarter for pleasantries, apparently, with the destruction of Earth and its Labyrinth at hand.

There was a rap at the door. Garritch and Slick came in.

William drew his gun.

The swiftness with which he did so startled Beatrice. She saw the tooled disdain with which the person he pointed it at responded and understood that this was the man William pursued. The man sensed Beatrice's scrutiny and winked at her, twisting a playful signal into something vile. She responded with a dry look of rebuttal.

Lark placed her hand gently on William's wrist. He flinched away from her, holstered his gun but kept his eyes on Slick. "We're not done."

"Anytime, pork belly. We can dance the merengue on a high wire."

"Not without my permission." Garritch tossed something shiny at William.

William caught it. Fia's bracelet—gold, but minus the gap.

"I'm afraid it won't work anymore."

Permission. Dog and master, these two. "Did he kill those people on your orders?" William asked Garritch, pointing at Slick.

"We needed information. To understand the nature of the danger that confronts us."

"He had to kill kids for that? A five-year-old girl?"

Garritch frowned and gave Slick a critical look. Sheer theater, William thought. Slick shrugged.

"Taking life was necessary," Garritch answered.

"No," Cabal said. "That was the way you chose. You did not know there was no other."

"We're out of time. I used the means available to me. My willingness to do that is why I am here. Absolve yourselves as you will. You knew I might employ such methods and did nothing to prevent me."

"*What* information?" William snarled.

"That which you possess," Garritch said.

"Someone *please* explain to me what this asshole is talking about."

"I did not go to the place of the killings to find you," Cabal told William.

William looked back and forth from Cabal to Garritch. "You were part of this?" he asked Cabal.

"I did not participate in the acts," Cabal said, "nor was I privy to them. Once they had been performed, I could not squander the opportunity to learn from them."

"Comes hard to you, doesn't it, explaining yourself."

"I knew of you from the monk Kawaguchi, and intended to seek you out. I did not know I would find you in the Crenshaws' apartment. It was fortuitous that I did. It is better for all of us that I remain objective and dispassionate, so I subjected you, instead of myself, to the young girl's *mors resonare*—her death echo. Of all who died there, hers was the strongest."

"That your bullshit idea of an apology for what you put me through?"

"No."

"You did that to yourself, smart guy, when you ran me out of town." Slick said. "That was *my* job."

"Your account would have been unreliable," Cabal told Slick. "You possess no empathy." Cabal gestured at William. "We require your report, Detective."

"My *report?*"

"Please describe for us, as clearly and succinctly as you can, what you experienced of the Crenshaw girl's death."

"You want to know what I felt?" William stabbed a finger in Cabal's granite chest. "Go back and feel it yourself. Take Itchy and Scratchy here with you." William wanted Slick to experience what he had. Repeatedly.

Lark touched his arm. "Please, Detective."

William stared at her. "*You* want this?" He didn't hear her response, distracted by a clarified perspective as he glanced around at the five other people in the room. The differences between them were so extreme it beggared comprehension. Whatever brought such angels and devils into alliance had to be terrible, which the memory he'd locked away, that they were so keen for him to describe, verified. William had never closed off a memory as he had the experience Cabal had subjected him to. Every time it started to leak into his thoughts, he'd met it with *no*, and kept meeting it, until doing so became reflex, as near to autonomic as he could manage. He'd built a wall of noes, an iron sphere. Within that enclosure was not just memory but cancer.

The destruction of Earth and its Labyrinth.

Beatrice observed that Lark was not above manipulating a man with her wiles. She did it with gentleness, according to her nature, not allure, but it was no less a seduction, and Beatrice liked her less for it, even recognizing that Lark did it with reluctance, pressed by extremity of need. A woman could not be so artful unpracticed.

Beatrice did not understand what Lark and Cabal were after. They had William caught between them, not physically but mentally and emotionally—Cabal direct, tactless and deadpan; Lark empathetic and encouraging—both pressing him to describe something he dreaded to revisit. This must have been what awakened him in Keel, the trauma he'd experienced before she first encountered him. Beatrice remembered the void at the center of the blind painter's mural. If William had come into but glancing contact with what she had sensed there, she could well understand his reluctance.

She wanted to stop them but was restrained by a terrible presentiment that this could not be shirked. Before they were done, this and more might be required of all of them. With the dubious exception of Slick, whose insouciance was surely feigned, there was desperation in everyone present—locked down in Cabal, suppressed in Lark, managed in Garritch, who stood aside with his arms crossed in frustration. It was terrifying to be among three such powerful people who were all so blighted with desperation.

William yielded—not to insistence or seduction. Some acquiescence moved him, a recognition like hers, Beatrice suspected, that this was all beyond him. The cost was apparent. He didn't pale, he changed color, his complexion taking a jaundiced cast. Beatrice feared to learn the nature of a memory that could assault one so. William staggered backward, collapsed into an armchair, described, in stuttering, broken phrases, being eaten alive inside. His voice rose, as if he had to shout to hear himself over an inner din. The memory was legion, murderous. Half incoherent, he strained to relate how what happened in his body happened also in his mind, his thoughts and memories ravaged, torn, mixed until they didn't connect with each other.

Beatrice moved to go to him. Cabal extended his hand, forestalling her. Something in the Hierophant's eyes was hard to look at. Like the history of the universe lived behind them.

William propped his head in his hand, calming his breathing, already at work, Beatrice recognized, re-containing the memory. She marveled at his will, that he could encyst such a thing in his psyche.

"Did the disruption go deeper?" Cabal asked William. "Deeper than your mind?"

"It went to the bottom of what I am," William answered, his voice rough from strain.

Cabal looked at Garritch.

William pushed the memory away. It stuck to the surfaces of awareness like poisonous glue. *No. No. No.* He took a deep breath and straightened in his chair. "Is that enough?" He glared at Cabal. "Get what you need? I could open a vein." *No. No. No.*

"*Liquori mortem*," Cabal said to Garritch. "We were right."

William swallowed, struggled to stop trembling. "What's that?"

"In crude terms the essence of death," Garritch said. "A substance which not only kills the body but literally destroys the soul, until now a thing only of arcane legend. We thought we knew what it was but could not analyze it. The only way to identify it was by its effect. The sample we had was residue from a place she has been."

William hadn't been sure that he had a soul, and now, apparently, it could be destroyed. "She?" He'd said that to Gan—*She's coming*—not knowing what he meant. Maybe now he would find out.

"I will show you both what we confront," Cabal said. He nodded at the unknown woman. "Close your eyes and still your thoughts."

"What are you doing?" William demanded. "I'm not going through that again."

"You will not," Cabal said. "I will show you, now, what *I* have seen."

Chapter Seventeen

William took a deep breath and nodded at Cabal, closed his eyes and braced himself, expecting to be battered.

A bright spot grew in his mind and opened like a dilating door. Stars reeled into view. He sling-shotted among them at impossible speeds, drew to a certain star around which planets orbited. William descended to one of the planets. Alien landscapes filled his mind. Armadas of plateaux in a bone-grey desert, an ocean with a nacreous, purple sheen, soaring mountains spanned by web-like rock formations. The trees looked dead. Everything looked dead. Everything *was* dead. A city, different from any human city, hive-like, crisscrossed by enormous looping structures, many broken, lying in rubble—multitudes of creatures lay motionless in what might have been streets. Limbs radiating from bulbous, oblong bodies. Dead, all of them, the ruins and corpses spattered with an inky substance William recognized. Life on the planet had been extinguished.

Beatrice's focus swam in on a particular corpse, on features that might have served senses or bodily functions, shriveled clusters of what might have been eyes. The vision took her through the eyes, into caverns like those she had traveled in the Labyrinth. More corpses were massed there. Stars showed through rents in the cavern walls.

The view spiraled out and traveled to another world vanquished by death and ruin, and then another.

The vision faded. Beatrice opened her eyes. The correct translation of the Aramaic pronoun for God acquired fresh significance. God surely had a multiplicity of faces if such beings were made in *Their* image. The Church had been right to establish a liaison with SETI. These reflections evaded the certitude that she would soon die. If not in the physical way commonly regarded as death, then by relinquishing who she was to become what was needed of her, surrendering to the will of a God she no longer knew.

"Tell them why, Cabal," Lark said.

William rested his head in his hand, again. Too many horrors for one day. Too many.

"It has long been my practice to consult, with regularity," Cabal said, "the oracle of the Labyrinth, concerning the general state of the human sphere. For some time, there have been portents of a danger approaching from beyond the Earthly domain. With Lark's help I explored outward into the firmament and discovered the worlds I have shown you laid waste. I also identified the entity responsible."

Cabal's bloodless demeanor chafed William. "Entity?"

"One possessed of hideous power."

William rubbed the inner left side of the bridge of his nose with the ring finger of his right hand. "What exactly do you want from me?"

"We want you to join us," Lark said.

"And do what?"

"We do not know the part you might play," Cabal said. "We know only that the Labyrinth has brought us together. It is possible that your investigative prowess may prove valuable."

"Prowess." William grunted. "I clear most cases out of sheer stubbornness."

"You evidence also a highly developed ethical sense."

"You want my ethical sense?" William aimed a finger at Slick. "Leave me alone with *this* guy for about twelve seconds."

Lark, Garritch and Cabal exchanged looks, seeming to consider it. For the first time William saw a hint of uncertainty cross Slick's face.

He remembered that look. It came to him that he had seen Slick before.

In Crenshaw's office, weeks before the murders, when William had been there to have two crowns seated. Following a dental assistant down the hall, he'd passed a room where Slick was in a dental chair with a paper bib clipped to his collar.

Wendy Crenshaw had been in her father's office that day, too. She'd been in Slick's room, telling him that her father was a good dentist and wouldn't hurt him.

"You were there." William leveled his gaze at Slick. "You were in Crenshaw's office, same day I was. I saw you talking to his daughter."

Slick's expression flattened.

"That's how you picked them, wasn't it? Bright, happy little girl trying to make *you* feel better. Impudent brat—who'd she think she was?" William stood up, watched Slick work to mask his discomfort. Everything fell into place. "You *hated* her, didn't you? Hated her cheerfulness and her innocence and how pampered she was." The fate of the world hanging in the balance, and the reasons for what had been done were banal and puerile. "Oh, yeah, you hated her. You hated her steady, upright parents for raising her to believe in good and think her life had value. Hated them for being good people. Just plain good people, and you hated that about them, didn't you? You wanted to rip that goodness right out of them and make them suffer. Show them what life's *really* like. You wanted to *corrupt* them, didn't you?"

Slick looked at nothing, his face set and expressionless.

William turned to the others. "You all do realize this guy is a psychopath, right?"

"He may yet prove useful," Garritch replied.

"Says the guy who sent him out to kill in the first place, leaving him to decide who, being too chickenshit to involve yourself in the choice, and making a show now of being willing to get your hands dirty."

Garritch averted his gaze.

Braden crossed to Slick in three strides, grabbed him by his shirt collar and put the muzzle of his gun hard in his left ear. "Go ahead, quicken; I'll go right the fuck with you. You think you can make something happen before I park one in your skull, try for it." He saw confidence drain from Slick. "Right about now you're wondering if I'm uncivilized enough to punch your brains all over the carpet of a good woman's living room. Or maybe I'll empty the clip right by your head, so you can hear church bells and train wrecks until the devil takes your rat-infested excuse for a soul as chum for the sharks of hell. Or maybe I'll leave you to ponder the day I'll find you and beat you until you blubber for mercy while I piss on your fucking wounds."

Lark touched William's arm. "Detective Braden …"

William shrugged her off with a growl and stomped outside to the balcony. Lark followed him. They stood awhile at the railing, gazing at the city in silence.

"We need Garritch," Lark said.

"Expect disappointment if you want me to be happy about that."

"He might not help us if you kill Slick."

"Then he's a complete fucking idiot, which I doubt, or you wouldn't want him. If you're right about what you've told me, he'd be screwing himself."

"True. But this is no time for dissension. And I think it ill-countenanced to initiate our venture with bloodshed."

"That's already happened!"

"Garritch acted independently. Contrary to his assertion, neither I nor Cabal can read his mind. We did not know what he had planned. That was not our entire company sanctioning murder."

William couldn't sort out his feelings.

"Why do you think he brought Slick with him?"

William gave her a sour look. "What, absolution?"

"Just so."

William grunted. "I don't get much sense of repentance from him."

"With what we have before us, none of us can afford to be distracted by either guilt or justice."

William leaned against the railing and hung his head. "Who am I kidding."

"You have nothing to fault yourself for."

"I had my chance. If I wasn't going to kill him then, I'm not going to now." He grimaced and looked at Lark. "Not that I'm proud of that."

Her eyes communicated understanding and a plea.

"I'm no executioner, lady, which that son-of-a-bitch knows. You don't have to worry. I don't understand what we're doing, here, though. The things that whacked-out bishop showed us—we're going to stop *that?* With what armies?"

"Armies will not defeat her."

"You all keep saying that—'her,' 'she.' One person did all of that?"

"She was an empress on a far world. What happened, how she became what she is, we do not know. All we know is that she drew terrible forces to her command and wields them without restraint. She believes in nothing. By which I do not mean that she holds no beliefs, I mean that that is an accurate characterization *of* her belief."

"And she's headed this way."

"Like a storm."

William let out a long sigh. "So, what's your plan? You must have a plan. Please don't tell me we're winging this."

"She would see a large force coming and destroy it. But a few people, if we can find a way to her, might be able to stop her."

"That's it? That's your plan?"

"Not entirely. There is a world whose Labyrinth is closely linked with ours. The beings there are very power-ful. They may be able to help us."

"And if they don't, or if they fail, it's just us."

"Yes."

"And if *we* fail—"

"The Earth dies."

William clenched the railing, hung his head and shook it again.

Lark gave his shoulder a stroke and went back inside, leaving him to his thoughts.

In the quiet, William noticed a faint trickling sound. He stepped over and touched the outer surface of the mineral column Lark's apartment occupied. His hand came back wet.

He sat down in an Adirondack chair, rolled a cigarette and lit it, tried to accommodate himself to the probability that the world was about to end. There were worse ways to go than trying to stop that, he supposed. He didn't doubt what he'd been told. They weren't lying to him. But he wished he could roll back time and not know about it. It was too big for him. He caught bad guys and put them away. Six people against a world killer? He should be running through the streets of Minuslitore, warning people, telling all the world leaders and generals on Earth. Except, of course, he had no way to do that, and who would believe him? What could they do? The best he might achieve would be giving a few locals bad dreams.

Six people. Two dodgy sorcerers, a couple of mysterious, winsome women, a murderer and a cop. If this was the Labyrinth's idea of an assault force, the Labyrinth was nuts.

The woman to whom William had not been introduced came out on the balcony through a far door. She leaned on the railing, looking out. It was too dark to see her face clearly. Nevertheless, William again had the impression that she was familiar.

He watched her, admiring her figure and how she held herself with her chin raised. Just the sight of this lovely creature was a balm to his soul. She was worth fighting for. She and every beauty life possessed.

Rage, rage, brother William, against the dying of the light.

She moved slowly in his direction, stopped about ten feet away, her face still in shadow. "I overheard you saying that you've become an archetype."

The voice—he knew that voice. "Hence the get-up." He gestured at his clothes. "I don't have to shop anymore. Step outside and my wardrobe is provided for me. Foomp." He snapped his fingers.

"That must be … strange."

"That's one word for it. I've got a few others. Say, have we met before?"

She didn't answer immediately, but leaned sideways against the railing, looking out. "Yes, William, we have met." She swayed upright and came still closer.

He could see her, now. Her eyes captured him. Somewhere, sometime, he'd seen those eyes.

William stood up. *"Beatrice?"*

Her smile broadened.

"How …"

"It seems the Labyrinth has a good effect on me."

He stared in amazement. "*Good* doesn't *begin* to cover it."

"William," she turned away, "don't look at me like that."

He averted his gaze. "Sorry. I just …" He had no idea what to say. "Have you become an archetype, too?"

"It seems not. Lark says the Labyrinth affects some people this way, restoring them to youth."

"Well, be glad. I mean, don't you think?"

"I don't know how I feel about it. Are you glad?"

"Of course I'm glad. It's wonderful. It's fantastic." He stopped, unsure what she'd meant. He cleared his throat. "I guess it must be … like you said, strange. How has it affected your …" He felt like an idiot.

"My vows?" Beatrice tapped the railing lightly with her fingertips. "I gave one life to the Order. I do not feel called to give another."

"That doesn't run contrary to your beliefs?"

Beatrice heard the hope in William's voice. He wouldn't admit it, probably not even to himself. But it told her what she needed to know.

"My beliefs live in me differently than they did." She looked out at the city. She had not asked all of the questions; she did not know all of the answers. "The core of my faith is unchanged." She could not have explained to herself how that remained true. "My beliefs are part of me, William. A surgeon couldn't cut them out. I love them. I do not think people should let the things they love be taken from them. Not if they can help it."

"Hey, I'm not trying to take anything from you."

"I know, William."

The way she looked at him then, with the light limning the chalice of her face, stilled every question and doubt in William's mind, and he knew that he had chanced into the path of grace.

Beatrice closed the distance between them, took William in her arms and kissed him.

Chapter Eighteen

Striding across the Endless Plain, Beatrice awakened. Acres long, her black habit streamed behind her. Her veil flared like a great hood housing her face; she gloried in the wind. Aqueous hues sparred in the heavens; sands swarmed and dervished below.

She had come to sue for passage, from whence to where she did not know. Not places but conditions of being. She had lived one way, as she had vowed, and determined now to live another.

Patches in the ground around her darkened. Water welled in her footprints. Metallic spikes, needle-like, poked up from the sands, joined to axe blades revealed in rising, mounted on long poles: golden halberds, myriad into the farthest distances, emerged forest-like from the Plain.

The surface of the Plain sank beneath deepening water, within which green life formed. Roots curled about Beatrice's feet; round leaves spread on the water's surface. Blooms opened in silent crescendo; the Plain exhilarated with water lilies.

Doors of innumerable kinds floated down from the sky and joined, frame to frame, into an endless, towering wall. Beatrice stopped to regard the impediment of options. A door directly before her, of weathered, rough-hewn wood, hung loose on its hinges, creaking in the wind. A plain door; a simple door. A door that sought no notice, but that, in its humble estate, was invisibly, unassailably sacred. A shepherd's door.

She pushed and the door yielded easily. Crossing the threshold, her great robes tattered into multi-colored shreds that dispersed like a cloud of butterflies.

Beatrice awakened, naked in bed, snug against William's back. She did not open her eyes but pictured him in her mind—his shoulder rising, soft and mountainous, the vulnerable, messy nape of his neck. She had travelled a lifetime to lie with this man, fulfilling, it felt, an older vow, not made of words, that stretched beyond all she knew.

It could so easily have gone any number of other ways, miracle it had not.

A fragment of dream came to her: roots growing to the contours of her immersed feet. Which took her to bathing with William, her head against his chest, water showering over them, rivulets streaming his skin—one she tracked with the pad of her finger along the ridge of his hip, recalling the taste of salt.

William stirred; Beatrice rolled onto her back as he shifted away. His weight pressed into the mattress to either side of her. She opened her eyes to find him staring down at her.

"Good morning." She stretched.

His gaze persisted.

"What?"

"I'm too old for you."

She laughed. "I don't believe you said that."

"I should be arrested."

"Do you hear yourself?"

"My ears work fine."

"You remember that I'm pushing ninety? And not in dog's years."

"Not anymore you're not."

She laughed again, beholding the wonder of him. "So, how ancient are you, Methuselah?"

"Forty-seven."

"I'm the one who should be arrested."

"I fell for you when you were still in your habit."

"Oh, now *that's* a pretty fiction."

"I mean it. When we left Keel, I felt like I was going the wrong direction because you weren't with me."

Beatrice remembered how she'd felt, watching the *Passenger* sail away. "You weren't alone in that. I'm glad we've found each other again, William."

He kissed her brow, her nose, her cheeks, her mouth. She stroked his face.

"Was I all right last night?" he asked.

"All right does not begin to cover it."

"Was that your first time?"

She frowned faintly and nodded.

"That's an honor I'll never live up to."

She rolled her eyes, patted his face, eased from under him and climbed out of bed. "I think we're both old enough to dispense with romantic foolishness. Particularly when the world is ending." She opened the curtains. The upper reaches of columns ranked through the distance outside.

"I'm smitten, I can't help it. You're going to have to put up with some foolishness." He loved the way she moved. He flopped on his side to watch her dress, winced and inhaled sharply.

"Are you all right?"

"Yeah. Just a little tender."

"Those bruises look awful."

"I'll heal. Faster with you around." He winked at her.

She grinned. "I'm glad you don't have to wear your superhero costume to bed."

"That's a relief, isn't it. Gan told me that when you're alone with someone you're close to you get to drop the impediments. At least ones that involve clothes."

"Thank God for small favors." She sighed. "Meanwhile, the world is ending."

"Stop saying that. It ain't gonna happen."

"You're sure, are you?"

He got up and held her face. "I have faith that we're going to stop it." He folded up the look she gave him and tucked it away in his heart.

He pulled on his pants. "You might have to get used to people calling me Bogie."

"Not truly."

"Seems that when you become an archetype you have to put up with being renamed by something like popular consensus. Unless you come up with a name on your own."

"Well, come up with one."

"Can't think of one I like. I confess no fondness for Bogie."

Beatrice sat back down on the bed. "Let's pick one together."

"Now?"

"No, when you grow up."

"I leave it to you."

"You want *me* to rename you?"

"Well, Bogie's the brainchild of a Wagnerian fat woman who parades around on a floating sofa and calls herself Crisis."

Beatrice stared at him.

"I could not make this stuff up. I owe her my life, in fact. She and her friends saved the ship."

"They have my gratitude. So, you want to accept 'Bogie' in her honor?"

"I'm willing to find another way to thank her."

Beatrice considered. "How about Sam?"

William's eyebrows rose. "I see where you're going. But Sam was the piano player."

"Wrong movie."

"Oh, yeah. Say, that fits. In more ways than one." He looked at his reflection in the mirror. "I could wear that."

"I hereby dub you Sam."

He grinned. "Sam it is, then."

There was a knock at the door. "Join us when you're ready," Lark called.

Sam left his hat on the dresser. It flew after him and settled on his head when he stepped from the room.

Garritch, Cabal and Lark waited in the living room.

"Where's Slick?" Sam asked.

"He is not party to this undertaking," Cabal said.

Sam presented Garritch with a biting grin.

"Draw close around me," Cabal said, disregarding Sam's ire.

They all gathered around the Hierophant.

A fog manifested, growing so dense that Beatrice could not see Sam standing next to her. When it cleared, they were in a green meadow suspended among the stars.

Nebulae, galaxies, planets and comets traveled about them in an unfathomable dance.

Gazing up into the phantasmagoric firmament and its manifold mysteries that bore no resemblance to the star-filled sky he knew, Sam began to understand what Lark had told him. He couldn't place himself in the scope of all this. The methods of investigative inquiry wouldn't serve. He had gone past theory, evidence and conclusion. If he were to understand anything, he would have to let the cosmos teach him.

In the center of the meadow stood a slender arch about ten feet tall that streamed with prismatic colors. Lark led the group to it. "Through this door," she said, "you can travel to the Labyrinths of other worlds, and to the Ur Labyrinth that spans the reaches between them. Other doors access Labyrinths and worlds beyond Earth, but none who have tried them have been known to return. No one understands why, but I think it may be because those doors are not anchored. This door *I* anchor."

Sam realized their number was dwindling yet further. "You're not going with us."

"I will be the beacon that guides you home. I will remain here and await your return."

"So, we're down to four."

"That is the number given," Cabal said.

"Given?"

"By the cards. In the heart of the Labyrinth is a cavern known as the House of Cards. In it is a wall of doors that is oracle to the Labyrinth."

"I went there," Beatrice said. "That was where I found my way to you."

Cabal nodded. "I sought there for a course of engagement with the power that threatens us. Four doors opened in answer to my query, and they all led here." He gestured at the gate.

Sam scratched the back of his head. If he stacked up all he understood of what he'd experienced since arriving at the Townsley Arms next to all he didn't, the latter would be the mountain. "All right." He let go of trying to understand.

"The place we go now is the Labyrinth of another world," Cabal said. "The beings whose aid we seek are not human but may seem familiar to you. Is everyone ready to proceed?"

"I've been ready," Garritch said.

Sam and Beatrice looked at each other. They nodded.

"Bring them home," Cabal told Lark.

She gave him a wary look. "I hold for you all." She rubbed her hands together and reached to touch his face.

Cabal backed away. "Do not expend yourself on my behalf." He stamped his staff on the ground, said, "*Aperire*," stepped through the arch and vanished.

Lark stared after him, with a heavy sigh turned to Garritch, who had moved before her.

She placed her hands on his face, covering his eyes with her palms. "Change your ways," she said and released him. Garritch responded with a recalcitrant smirk and followed Cabal.

"What's that about expending yourself?" Sam asked.

Lark placed her hands on Beatrice as she had Garritch, said something Sam didn't understand and released her.

She reached out to Sam. A radiant warmth poured into him when she placed her hands on his eyes. "Trust intuition more than logic," Lark said and released him.

Sam held her gaze, getting that she had no easy task before her, either.

Beatrice took his hand and they faced the gate together. She had spent the greater decades of her life treading the same familiar ground, until she knew every path, every step, every view in her circumference. Now, in a period of time minuscule by comparison, she had traveled beyond the limits of dreams, until nothing was familiar but the man beside her, whom she felt she had known forever.

Sam and Beatrice stepped through together. In a single stride they left Lark's celestial meadow and passed from one reality to another.

Chapter Nineteen

The cavern floor was irregularly crisscrossed by deep crevasses, the ground hard and rough, grown in spots with moss-like vegetation. In the heights above, arched openings perforated unscalable stone walls in irregular rows. Winged creatures stood in some of the archways and flew about the upper reaches of the cavern. They looked small as sparrows in the distance, but it was clear they were much larger.

"Are those *dragons?*" Sam asked in wonder.

"They are called that on Earth," Cabal said. "Here, in their own tongue, they call themselves simply, 'the people.'"

Sam surveyed the terrain around them. He stepped to the brink of a nearby crevasse. It plummeted to black depths and was too wide to jump across. "I don't know where we're going, but I don't think we're getting there on foot." He saw a dragon swoop low and head toward them, reached for his gun.

Cabal leaned his staff against Sam's chest. "Adopt an attitude of submission."

Beatrice took Sam's hand. The dragon came straight at them, its face a mosaic of scales and horny protrusions, its eyes steady and fierce. It drew its feet forward, scooped up Beatrice and Sam in one, Cabal and Garritch in the other, arced about the way it had come, flapped its wings and climbed.

Beatrice and Sam strained against each other for room to breathe. The dragon's grip tightened. Beatrice understood what was happening, found Sam's hand and squeezed it. "Stop struggling."

Sam mastered his panic and went still. The dragon's hold on them loosened.

"Holy shit."

"We're being carried through the air by a dragon," Beatrice said in amazement.

"Yeah, I failed to miss that."

The curled perimeter of the dragon's foot was a little ahead. Beatrice squirmed toward it.

"What are you doing?" Sam asked.

"I want to see!"

Her hair blew back as her head cleared the opening. Sam worked himself up beside her. The dragon's wings made a slow, steady *whump*; the walls of the alien Labyrinth blurred past. From on high the broken floor of the cavern looked crazed.

Beatrice sensed Sam watching her. There was admiration in his eyes.

"You're enjoying this, aren't you?" His hat flew off. He looked up after it. "Well, there goes that."

Abruptly, they were in a different cavern, where a broad river wound along the floor amid rolling grasslands and forests of purple trees. The scene changed again to a drier environ, where herds of kangaroo-like creatures hopped about over yellow grasslands. One of the creatures jumped haplessly into the mouth of a swooping dragon. And then they were flying through clouds above emerald seas.

"He's quickening through his Labyrinth!" Beatrice cried.

"Giving us the tour, you think?" Sam noted that his hands were smaller than the scales on the dragon's knuckles.

Beatrice laughed. "I don't know, but it's thrilling!" This was how she wanted to live, with the wind in her teeth, side by side with the man she loved. She kissed Sam on the cheek.

With her hair blown back in the rushing air, and her eager eyes taking in everything, Sam fell in love with her again. "You're a wild one, Beatrice Cloutier."

She beamed. "Complaining?"

"Not one bit."

Beatrice kissed him again, on the lips. She nodded at Garritch and Cabal. "They don't look happy."

Sam couldn't help laughing. Two worse-suited travel companions were hard to imagine. Cabal was placid as ever, Garritch the picture of displeasure.

Sam yielded to the spirit of adventure. He might not have done so without Beatrice at his side, and he knew it. She snuggled against him. They flew above lakes, past aeries with elaborately sculpted entrances, through a cavern that seemed entirely composed of mammoth blue crystals. Sam noticed something about quickening. The name was misleading. They weren't going faster, they were passing through a series of invisible portals of some kind. Which begged the question, did you have to know where the portals were, or did they come to you? Reviewing his experiences, the latter seemed more likely.

The dragon quickened a final time, and they entered a cavern more wondrous than the rest. Forests of many colors climbed the arching walls high to either side, waterfalls piled down cliff faces that looked hewn by titanic axes. Some of the trees were tall as skyscrapers. Dragons perched in their branches.

Built out from the right wall of the cavern was a behemoth palace, columns hundreds of feet high lining a sprawling dais, beneath which myriad terraces extended, all fashioned from cyclopean stone. On the terraces lush, wild gardens grew around deep blue pools. Two great waterfalls spilled from the roof of the dais major, feeding, through sundry channels, the pools of the terraces, and ultimately a great lake at the bottom, in the cavern floor. Some of the pools on the terraces steamed, and dragons basked within them.

Beyond the grand palace was an immense grotto, where other palatial constructions crowded the cavern walls. It seemed they had entered a dragon city.

Many dragons were gathered on the dais major, standing or lounging on enormous stone benches. At the back of the dais a dragon markedly larger than the rest, its skin bright with myriad colors, sat curled on a massive, throne-like pediment extending from the cavern wall.

The dragon who bore them released the humans to the floor of the dais major in front of the throne. Sam stumbled from its grasp and Beatrice helped him to his feet just as his hat spun down and secured itself on his head. Garritch grumbled and cursed, indignant at having been transported thus.

Cabal alone seemed unruffled or diminished in poise. He approached the throne and took a knee. Other dragons gathered around the group, towering above them. "Lord Gyralon, King of the Hidden Aeries, Keeper of the Forgotten Flame, Knight of the Bloom Eternal, and Protector of the Traveling Veils, thank you for granting us audience."

"Do you seek to beguile me with solicitude, Cabal?"

"I tender respect, Your Majesty, and intend no offence."

"Your purpose is known to us."

"Then you know our cause is dire."

"Your cause is lost. The Empress is upon you. We can but offer your company refuge to live out your time."

"We do not yield to despair, Sire. We seek your alliance."

"You seek the sacrifice of thousands, perhaps millions of our kind, and come with only four."

"We advance, Sire, according to the designs of our Labyrinth. Any force we might muster would fail as dust before the Empress. Yours is the only kind we know who can stand against her. We propose only that you draw her attention while we enter her keep and attempt to destroy her."

"Attempt, yes, and likely fail."

"We are prepared to lose our lives in the effort."

"And legions of ours as well."

"She will not avoid you forever, Lord Gyralon. She gains power with each world she takes. If she continues as she has, she may graduate to consume galaxies. She seeks the end of the universe."

"She will fail long before she consumes the worlds in this galaxy alone. It is in the nature of her madness that she blinds herself to the futility of her objective. It is likely that she will exhaust herself before she turns her gaze upon us. She knows we would not fall easily."

"Perhaps, Sire, you understand her art better than I. I do not believe there is much of *her* left. She is become a juggernaut, possessed of a single intent. At what remove does she cease to be stoppable? How many worlds have fallen already? Hundreds? Thousands? You know better than I. The universe is not yet open to us as it is to you. How many trillions, or millions of trillions of souls disintegrate inexorably in the abomination she has created? Do we abandon them because they lived other lives on other worlds? Beneath flesh we are travelers in kind."

"He is right, Gyralon," a voice said. The circle of dragons parted. An elder dragon limped forward. Her scales had gone grey; her eyes were rheumy, her voice raspy. "A violence so terrible cannot be met with complacency."

"Let her burn herself out, Isakell. The souls she takes can be mended afterwards."

"We do not know that she *will* burn out. Nor is it certain that the souls she has claimed can return to wholeness. Their number is already beyond imagining, and the thing she has made will continue to wreak havoc even after she expires."

"I will not subject our people to senseless slaughter to save a single world. If we are to confront the Empress, we need to prepare."

"Prepare how? Study the signs? Consult the oracles? There is no strategy equal to this enemy. We have studied and consulted enough to know that. Here are four courageous souls with a daring plan—"

A terrible noise, like a gargantuan expulsion of steam and rending of stone, interrupted Isakell. The dragons all scrambled to the edge of the dais, the humans following.

Across the vast grotto, the palatial structures carved in the walls shook from the exertion of a force in the rock behind them, causing streams of sand to spill from their seams and crevices and the beetled cliffs above them. A palace at the center of the agitation collapsed, its broken columns and terraces plummeting to the cavern floor, sending up enormous clouds of dust. The cavern ceiling above the destruction cracked, loosing massive plates of rock that rode down upon dragons flying beneath them and bore them to their deaths.

In the cavity left by the sundered palace, rock splintered and broke apart in a concentric progression of collapse. That entire end of the grotto then fell, roof and all, with a deafening din, the shockwave blowing both dragons and humans back from the verge of the royal dais and tumbling across its floor.

Sam struggled to his feet and fought his way blindly through dust-filled air in search of Beatrice. He stumbled across a body, helped Garritch to his feet and searched on. The dust thinned and he spotted her. She was shaken and disoriented but able to stand.

There was a tear in the sleeve of her jumpsuit and a scrape on her arm. Sam looked around for something to use as a bandage, started to take off his trench coat.

Beatrice stopped him. "I'm fine, Sam. I'll be fine." She pointed outward through the clearing air.

In the collapsed end of the cavern there was now an enormous breach, the area within its perimeter filled by a grey oscillation, the composition of which was indiscernible. It possessed within its makeup a slow rotation which advanced with an aspect of purpose.

Dragons leapt into flight throughout the cavern, flew toward the encroaching phenomenon and assaulted it with fire. Their attack had a worse than failed effect. The eldritch field churned forward, broadening its zone and consuming its assailants, none of whom emerged from its grip.

Gyralon came to the edge of the dais and bellowed a command. The dragons following after their fellows turned from their advance and amassed before him. Isakell came beside Gyralon and let forth a steady sound from her throat, a single, clear tone almost too deep for human hearing. The other dragons took up her song, and advanced through the grotto, fanning out in formation to meet the oncoming cataclysm with a wall of sound.

Sam stared at the maelstrom, suppressing his fear. There was something in it he needed to see. Within its makeup something writhed, like a beast trying to make itself out of alienated elements. Trying to *become*, in ignorance of what it was, to wrest consciousness from chaos.

But in the center of that chaos was another thing, a transparent sphere, like a bubble. Within that capsule Sam perceived a figure, dragon-like, with wings and a long neck.

It looked at him.

He couldn't see its eyes but he could feel its scrutiny, tendrils snaking through his mind. The tendrils found his sequestered memory and teased it. The figure transformed, and Sam saw it more clearly. It had a human semblance, now, female, possibly, clothed in long, black robes.

The singing dragons increased in number, thousands quickening into the grotto to reinforce their fellows, until they were so many that the maelstrom was obscured from view.

The four humans drew together. They couldn't hear each other over the dragons' chant. Sam and Beatrice held each other.

The song relented and the dragons dispersed from their formation. The breach in the cavern was sealed by a grey, featureless wall, like a monstrous bandage, that did not match the colorations of surrounding stone nor emit any lumination.

Isakell loomed over the human group, urgency in her eyes. "You must leave."

"We cannot retreat," Cabal said. "If we return to the gate of our crossing, all is lost. We will never find the

Empress' keep, nor have any hope of contest. Our world, our Labyrinth, will be consumed."

"Then you have no other choice than to quicken into the Ur. You cannot stay here. Gyralon will close the doors around you and you will be killed."

"We did not cause this," Cabal objected.

"You do not know that. Can you prove it, even to yourself? None of us can be certain where she is concerned. We do not know how she perceives or what she sees. Perhaps she sensed a threat from you and came here to deter you. The damage you see is not restricted to this cavern. It extends throughout our Labyrinth, and even to the surface of our world. Thousands, possibly millions, have died this day, and their souls now disintegrate in her cauldron of madness. You will be blamed. You must escape into the Ur."

For the first time Cabal's expression marred with futility. "The chance of finding a way to her from the Ur is infinitesimal."

"Will you refuse an infinitesimal chance if it is the only one you have?" Isakell looked over her shoulder. "Gyralon has closed the doors around you. I hold open the door to the Ur—he has not considered that way. But you must go now. Once he is here you are lost."

Sam noticed black splotches on the mended wall and wanted to warn the dragons about them, but Cabal gestured to the others and they gathered close. He stamped his staff on the stone floor of the dragon king's dais major. A fog enveloped them again. When it cleared, they were in a realm of reflections.

Chapter Twenty

They stood upon no certain ground.

They had quickened into a tunnel that stretched indefinitely in both directions, more or less round in its bore, maybe thirty feet in diameter. It was difficult to gauge its dimensions with infinities of reflections surrounding them in innumerable degrees of inclination. The surfaces of the tunnel possessed the irregularities of a natural cave, but eccentrically shaped mirrors adhered to their contours like crystalline facets.

Garritch sat down in an attitude of defeat. "What have you done to us, Cabal?"

Cabal took in their surroundings without responding.

"Are we trapped?" Sam asked.

"Lark holds the gate for us," Cabal said, "but to return now is to accept doom."

"Yes, yes," Garritch said, "she holds the gate. But we need a door to get there, and I don't find one, do you?"

"Not in the immediate vicinity. I'm not looking for that door."

Garritch laughed helplessly. "You cling to the fantasy that we can defeat her. The four of us. Did you *see* what she did to the dragons? You're insane."

"Hey," Sam said to Garritch, "I'd rather die fighting. What are we looking for?" he asked Cabal.

"I'm not sure. I know how to go, but not where to go. Or maybe it's the other way around."

"You're the detective," Garritch said. "Detect, why don't you? Find us a way out of here."

"All right let's try that. Clue me in about these doors. You want to go someplace, one comes to you, right?"

"Essentially, yes," Cabal said.

"So, we want to go someplace. What's the problem?"

Garritch sighed. "The doors are drawn to travelers, people who can quicken."

"Ain't that us?"

"Yes, but we're probably the first of the Quick to come to this place, which means doors have never been drawn here. We don't know where we are. The nearest doors might be millions or trillions of miles from here. Light years. If there were one near enough to summon, I would know. I would feel it. Trust me, I'm good at it. Maybe even better than him." Garritch gestured at Cabal.

Sam thought. "But any door can take you anyplace, right? I could step into a door in Schenectady and step out here, yes?"

"No. Within the earthly domain, the Earth and its Labyrinth, yes, any door can take you anywhere. Once you know how to summon them. There are exceptions, but they're irrelevant. Only a relative handful of doors access the stars."

"How many?"

"No one knows, exactly, but not many."

"How do you tell which are which?"

"You can't. It's your intent that draws one to you."

"Not all doors travel," Cabal said. "Some are stationary, bound by either place or potential."

"You two talk like they're alive."

"No." Garritch shook his head emphatically. "Someplace where there's a lot of activity, like a city, or maybe a town, it generates possibilities. Sometimes a door settles into those possibilities; no one knows why. There's a theory that the stationary doors anchor the traveling ones. But the doors aren't alive."

"That's not certain," Cabal said.

Garritch made a face. "They're not alive."

"So, the only place doors become stationary is cities or towns?" Sam asked.

"It can happen in other places," Cabal said.

Beatrice reached out to touch her reflection in a small, irregularly heptagonal mirror. It was difficult to tell how the mirrors were oriented. Her fingers touched glass and her reflection warped and multiplied. She caught her breath, peered both ways into distances. Not all of the mirrors were secured to the walls. Some floated about, drifting lazily through the air. Beatrice saw a mirror detach from a spot and levitate in such a fashion, noticed others settle against walls and adhere to them. The cavern was in a state of fluctuation. "We're looking for a way to the Empress?"

"Yes," Cabal said.

"And this—" Beatrice continued looking around—"*place* connects Labyrinths … related to worlds …" She wasn't sure how to frame the question.

"Wherever imaginative consciousness emerges, so, too, a Labyrinth of some nature," Cabal said. "Here, we are between Labyrinths."

"No man's land," Sam said.

"So to speak," said Cabal.

"Well—" Beatrice frowned at a mirror that reflected her face in profile—"if we don't know where we are, and we don't know where to look, one way's as good as the other, isn't it?"

"What are you thinking?" Sam asked.

"We've only got two options; why don't we take a vote? Or flip a coin?"

"There is a third option," Cabal said.

"What?" Sam asked.

"Stay put," Garritch said, "and wait for the magic to happen."

Sam wanted to swat him. "Try keeping the sarcasm to yourself. So, sometimes doors become stationary in places other than cities or towns. Where and why?" he asked Cabal.

"Impossible to know where until one becomes stationary. As for why, they are drawn by potentials."

"What kind of potentials?"

"Unknown."

"But if there were one of these stationary doors around here, you'd feel it?" Sam asked Garritch.

"You can't sense a stationary door. Precisely because it's stationary."

"Well, what good are they? Who's gonna use something they can't find?"

"They're not used much," Garritch said, "but the locations of most of them are known. They develop a physical aspect when they become stationary. You can see them. Like Lark's archway."

"Okay, right there—you say the circumstances that might result in a door becoming stationary are unknown, but you call that 'Lark's archway.' Did she make that or find it?"

"Both," Cabal answered.

Garritch scrunched his face. "*Sort* of. That's a unique case."

A unique case was exactly what Sam wanted. "So, let me get this straight. We know there are no traveling doors around here because neither of you can sense any."

"Right," Garritch said.

"But there could be a stationary door that you don't sense."

Garritch shook his head.

"Why not? We're a potential, aren't we? Being here?"

"Think about what you're saying. We quickened at random into the Ur Labyrinth, which extends throughout the universe, connecting Labyrinths."

"We don't know that," Cabal said.

"Whatever." Garritch waved the comment away. "The point is, its length is infinite or as good as. Some door reacted to a potential that we four might come to this specific spot at some indeterminate time and settled in to wait for us?"

"It is possible," Cabal said.

Garritch smirked. "Like it's possible a herd of unicorns might come trampling through here."

Beatrice heard something and disconnected from the exchange. She stilled her mind and closed her eyes, identified a sound. The cave hummed faintly, almost inaudibly: the A above middle C. She felt it in her skin, and at the base of her spine. She could feel her companions, too—zones of presence in a far greater presence. Reverberations within a field. Garritch was a chord of fear masked by cynicism. Cabal was a more complex chord, unyielding by ancient habit. Sam was a fiery overture of defiance.

The three men stopped talking. Beatrice opened her eyes to find them watching her.

She fixed on Sam and said, "Seek."

He frowned.

"Still your mind and seek." *And may the Mother of Christ guide you.*

Sam straightened, holding her gaze. He relaxed his shoulders and became observant, went into investigative mode. He stepped to the cave wall and studied reflections.

He saw himself, near and far, from every angle—from the back, too, maybe reflected from across the cave. He saw his companions multiplied.

Between their reflections he noticed slivers of things not present. He looked both ways down the tunnel. Irregularly shaped mirrors, from minuscule to large, adhering at odd angles—how far might a reflection travel, glancing from wall to wall …

"They're not all reflections."

The others looked at him.

Sam pointed upward. "See that little rectangular piece? That's not us or anything around us. Looks like trees."

He started left but then went right, following instinct, moving slowly, searching for things out of place. The more he looked, the more he saw. The others murmured confirmation.

Garritch pointed. "There's a building there."

Fragments and shards of other worlds, other Labyrinths, minuscule windows too limited to make anything out clearly—

"Mountainside, maybe."

"Road."

"Sky."

Sam wasn't looking for those things. Something moved above him. A trapezoidal piece of glass floated past—not a mirror, a window—in its boundary an oscillating field.

"There!" he pointed. "Follow that. Don't lose it."

They scrambled after the floating window, their own reflections preceding them kaleidoscopically down the tunnel.

Sam lost sight of it. "Where'd it go?"

"There!" Beatrice pointed.

The trapezoidal window secured itself to the left wall, displacing two mirrors that swooped down the way the group had come, making Garritch duck.

The party gathered around the window. The oscillating field that filled it was unmistakable. It was the maelstrom, in a somewhat more quiescent state, that had attacked the dragons' realm.

"It isn't a door," Garritch muttered.

"Yeah, so we should probably ignore it." Sam studied the surrounding mirrors. Among them were a disproportionate number of windows, showing places and things both strange and familiar, and most definitely not present in the cave.

"You believe in signs now, Detective?" Garritch was back to sarcasm.

"I go where evidence takes me." Sam pointed at the anomalous facets. "I'll bet there's a little bit of everywhere, here." He noticed a reflection of the wall behind him, turned around. "Sweet Mother of Jesus."

They crossed the cave together. On the far wall, four, identical, oblong windows, holding to the wall vertically, showed views of the Empress' deranged maelstrom. The windows were about six feet tall.

Terrible, the view they presented, sickening to the instincts, not for what was visible, but for the unanswerable implications.

"Those are souls?" Sam asked.

"Riven to pieces," said Cabal.

"They look atomized."

"Very nearly. What you're seeing is not the souls themselves but the agitation of ether. They are trying to find themselves."

The particles in the chaotic volume, whatever their nature, were in pain. Sam had experienced the loss of self they fought. "Is it just me, or are these things shaped like coffins?"

"I was wrong to doubt you, Detective," Garritch said. "You have found our doors."

"Door," Cabal corrected. "Only one." He pointed. In the middle right window an impression of place could be seen amid the rabid oscillations: archways, stairs, a great hall. "The Empress' keep. The others lead to ruin." Cabal placed his hand on the glass and raised his staff to stamp it.

"Hold on," Sam said. "Shouldn't we have a plan?"

Without reply Cabal brought down his staff. This time his quickening fog formed only around him. It dispersed and he was gone.

"Great. Now what do we do?"

"Follow him," Garritch said. "This threshold we cross each on our own." He extended his hand toward the glass and bowed to Beatrice. "Milady?"

She gave Garritch a tired look and stepped toward the glass.

"Beatrice, wait."

She turned her kind, warming gaze on Sam. "We can't prepare for the unknown, William Braden. We can only meet it with all that we are." She made the sign of the cross, placed her hand on the glass, and closed her eyes. Sam felt like he lost a piece of himself when she disappeared.

Garritch again extended his hand and nodded to Sam.

"No, that's all right, you go ahead."

Garritch grinned, casually touched the glass and vanished.

Sam was alone again. He couldn't see the others, just the same uncertain impression of architecture through a fog of agony. He swallowed and hummed, deep in his throat, placed his hand on the glass and wished himself where Beatrice was.

Chapter Twenty-one

The place was like the underbelly of an old castle, everything built of stone, from the walls to the vaulted ceilings. The light was grey and diffuse, its source unclear. Crypts stood here and there, featureless effigies recumbent upon their lids. A coffin leaned upright by an arched entry to a larger space.

"Are we inside the bubble?" Sam asked.

The Hierophant scanned their surroundings. He went through the archway by the coffin. The others followed him into an immense round chamber with a lofty domed ceiling. To the right a stone stairway with no bannister climbed the curved wall to a high door. Cabal led them up the stairs.

At the door he stopped. "She is near."

No one responded. They all felt it, an insidious enervation penetrating their bones.

Cabal opened the door.

They entered a vast rectangular chamber and stopped, out of uncertainty and trepidation, but a few steps in. The place, illuminated by flaming braziers, had the feel of a great temple. The mammoth Doric columns lining the length of its perimeter reminded Beatrice of the Parthenon. But this was no ruin, nor was it faithful to any site on Earth. Where the statue of Athena would have stood, instead a giant, six-armed, sword-wielding goddess figure reminiscent of Kali towered over them, wearing a pharaonic crown with a cobra on its brow. The wall at the far end of the temple was black as purest darkness.

"This is all whim," Garritch said. "Preparation for her assault on Earth."

"Not all." Cabal gestured at the other walls.

The temple was also an ossuary. The walls behind the colonnades and the statue were covered with the bones of a multitude of life forms, joined and articulated against their original designs to create a grotesque impression of unity. Garritch became absorbed with the assembly of the wall left of the doorway.

Beatrice did not know how the temple had come into being, but of one thing she was certain: it made her feel small.

A low vibration passed through the floor with a pulsating rhythm.

"Garritch," Cabal called.

Garritch was still preoccupied with the wall, tracing connections between bones. "This is ingenious."

"It is madness," Cabal said.

"Mad genius. I think it's a mechanism."

"Garritch!"

Garritch turned.

"She comes."

The vibration rose in intensity and became audible, like a distant siren with a volcanic voice. Arcing electricity scaled up the black wall, erasing the blackness to reveal the maelstrom, until oscillating chaos, restrained by an invisible barrier, filled that end of the chamber.

The pulsing noise rose to a deafening roar, augmented by a blaring clamor an octave higher, like a note played by a battalion of horns. The bones on the walls began to move, shifting and traveling with a purpose.

A figure emerged from an entry near the oscillating wall of the maelstrom. She did not appear fearsome but emanated cataclysmic presence. A long black gown she wore, that gleamed in firelight with ornate traceries of profane embroidery suggestive of creatures in torment. Bare above a white fur collar, her shoulders and neck described youth and a graceful bearing. Her hands as well, extending from the fur cuffs of her sleeves, seemed gentle and sensitive. She wore a skullcap, from the crown of which a great headdress bloomed, cascading upwards and curling around the sides of her face with shimmering black and white patterns like a fountaining fractal. A veil covered her eyes, with a slit for her nose, below which only her lips and chin showed, the latter implying the visage of a comely maiden.

Pure deception—abominable power poured from the creature. Sam felt like he was on the deck of the *Passenger* again, facing the onslaught of a storm.

The veil was a deception too. She did not need eyes to see. She had but one eye, and they were inside of it. Her eye looked inward upon them, pressing them with terrible curiosity. How, she wanted to know, had they penetrated her keep?

Her voice rumbled through them, not only in their hearing but all of their senses, and it was in their senses more than their minds that they understood her. She did not speak to them but revealed her convictions and intent, the incessant, churning, murderous determination to *be* the fate of all things. All would end; the eons of rise and struggle and creation would come to naught, serving no purpose but to expire and be forgotten, for there would be no one left to remember. The promise of the soul was a lie, another senseless prolongation of an existence without aim.

She would not wait. She embraced the end she envisioned and sought to hasten it. She wanted to be there at the final moment, take all and everything with her in one last orgasm of failure.

She was not a person, anymore; she was Armageddon personified.

Beatrice, stricken with fear as she was, sensed self-deception. Fanaticism encompassed them like a fever, a physical emanation from both the place and the Empress, a mad flight from truth.

But Beatrice did not know what truth that might be. She did not know what she was doing here, what function she might fulfill in resisting such monstrosity. Nothing in her, no faith, no belief, no understanding, no skill was equal to this foe. As the fourth member of their group she was dead weight.

One thing came to her that she did know how to do: abjure despair. If she possessed no other power with which to contest this adversary, she could do that.

And she could pray.

Cabal stepped toward the eldritch being, and Garritch joined him. Together they met the Empress' power with arcane gestures and spells, the words of the latter lost to the siren din. For the first time Sam saw something of worth in Garritch.

The Empress' head cocked upward; she sensed something she did not recognize. Her cacophonous siren song dimmed and fell silent; she did not understand why. Cabal and Garritch advanced on her, their words now audible, though understandable to neither Beatrice nor Sam.

The Empress bent. Her arms tightened to her sides, her entire figure contorted by invisible constriction.

She straightened and cast her arms wide. The siren din resumed at louder volume, accompanied by a searing blast of heat. Garritch, Cabal, Beatrice and Sam were blown backwards. Cabal slammed into a column and went still. Beatrice collided headfirst with the pedestal supporting the sculpture of pharaonic Kali and was knocked unconscious as well.

Sam and Garritch struggled to their feet. Sam drew his gun. He was sweating so much it nearly slipped from his hand. He got a grip on it and charged the Empress, fired until the clip was empty. The Empress seized him, not with her hand but an eldritch force, and bore him aloft, kicking and cursing in midair. Sam holstered his gun and pulled out Slick's, but it slipped from his grasp and fell to the floor. The Empress drew him close, snarling at him, brought him an inch from her face, the door of a blast furnace. A black, slimy, serpentine tongue emerged from between her pretty lips and slithered over his face.

Beatrice came around just in time to see the Empress cast Sam into the maelstrom of souls. She stifled a cry. Shouting for Cabal, Garritch battled the Empress on his own. Beatrice didn't know how he withstood her. He seemed to be inventing magic, searching for a weakness. It wasn't working but she wasn't overpowering him. She would; there was no question. The bone walls shifted and clattered wildly.

Beatrice crawled to Cabal and shook him. His face streamed with sweat. He blinked his eyes open and sat up.

"Where is the detective?"

"She cast him into her madness."

Beatrice helped Cabal to his feet.

He wiped sweat from his eyes, licked his thumb and made the sign of the cross on Beatrice's forehead. "Sleeper awaken," he said, holding her gaze. Then he turned and ran. He passed Garritch, ignoring his cries for help. Beatrice thought he was charging the Empress, but he ran past her too.

Sam fell through the churning cauldron of disintegrating souls, whose particles tore at each other all around him like hysterical ants. He was relieved to be free of the heat, but the relief was short-lived. He couldn't breathe, and the unity of his consciousness drew the souls to attack him, seeking themselves. His body defended him only partly, and he felt his psyche begin to yield, bits of memory and identity wrested from him. He knew he wouldn't last long.

Then another presence was with him. Cabal enveloped him in a sphere of immunity and Sam could breathe again. They held face to face, while the sphere buffeted through the maelstrom.

"Raise your weapon," Cabal said.

Sam held his gun extended. Cabal closed his eyes and spoke words Sam couldn't hear. Particles from the chaos attached to the exterior of the protective sphere and emitted tiny sparks. The sparks penetrated the bubble and collected on the surface of Sam's gun, clinging to it and bonding with its metal. The gun grew hot in Sam's hand.

"Maintain your grip, no matter the pain."

The pistol grew red hot, then white hot, and Sam held it, his eyes fixed ahead, his focus inward, meeting pain on its own ground, crying out in defiance as he needed.

The gun cooled and the pain receded. Sam breathed. He discovered his Glock 19 had transformed into a Colt revolver. He looked at Cabal, mystified.

"She will no longer be immune," Cabal said. He shoved Sam hard in his chest.

Sam was thrown out of the protective sphere. He watched Cabal sink away from him in his life bubble until he was lost in the churning wretchedness. The maelstrom's oscillations pivoted Sam slowly about. He saw where he was headed and cocked his gun, just before he passed through another barrier and returned to the Empress' temple of horrors.

❧

Beatrice watched in disbelief as Cabal plunged into the maelstrom. She had no attention to spare for distress; a change had begun in her. Cabal had summoned something forth from her depths—the core of who she had been and who she had become, bound in a nameless expression. She needed to cooperate, somehow, with the change, but Garritch was on his knees, struggling to fend off the Empress' malignity, near his last, and the Empress turned her eye on Beatrice with a force so terrifying and confounding it held Beatrice paralyzed in mind and body. Nothing mattered in the path of that scrutiny; no meaning, no purpose, no belief. All would lose themselves to mindless, selfless eternity, now or later, it mattered not. Better to sleep and join the still and seamless dream of eternal nothing.

No. By strain of will Beatrice looked away. Within the maelstrom something traveled, coalesced, acquired form. Beatrice cried out in joy to see Sam fly forth with his gun drawn, his trench coat flapping about him.

Sam fell, rolled to his feet and, in an instant, took in the scene. Cabal was gone, Garritch near spent in his contest with the monster, Beatrice relieved to see him but helpless. Sam shot the Empress in the back and kept firing, fanning his newly minted revolver by instinct. She screamed like the hounds of hell in chorus, and her human form flew apart into a thrashing mass of flailing limbs, not of one species but many, held together by her terrible will.

Sam couldn't tell where the vital parts were, so he fired at center mass. He shot six rounds, but the gun kept firing, magically possessed, now, it seemed, of inexhaustible ammunition.

The thrashing thing the Empress had become seized Sam by the throat with a limb, not tentacle, not arm, nor any particular thing, but a morphing mutation of many, and bore him aloft. Still he kept firing and still she screamed, but the bitch wouldn't die.

She restrained him, pinning his arms to his sides so he couldn't point the gun at her, and wrapped a tentacle around his head. He felt her probing his mind, more intimately than before, and with a purpose more clearly honed. The thing didn't care about his thoughts and made no effort to read them. It was looking for something else, some connection. She touched something that stirred a sense memory of warm hands on his eyes.

Sam realized that she was looking for Lark. Lark and the gate she anchored. The thing wanted to ride his connection to Lark straight back to its source. And worse, she wanted to absorb a power Lark possessed and twist it to her own designs.

Sam gritted his teeth, resisting her, summoning sense memories of his mother's embrace, of swinging a bat, the sound of the bat hitting his father's head, music, beer, laughter, pain, disgust for things he had seen. He couldn't divert her long. She would find what she was looking for.

Sam had an answer for that. *You want to dig in my head, baby, I've got a nugget for you.*

"Hey!" he shouted. A grotesquerie of optics fixed on him. Sam opened the sequestered memory of Wendy Crenshaw's death and let it fill his mind.

The thing hadn't expected that. She didn't like it and she didn't want it, so he fed it to her. She withdrew her tentacle from around his head. Her clamorous accompaniment died. She waved morphing appendages around the liquid wad her head had become, trying to fend off what he'd given her.

"Yeah," Sam said.

The Empress contorted, quivered, staggered, Sam lolling in her grasp.

"Yeah!" Sam worked his arm free but didn't bother to fire. The acid memory was doing better than bullets. *"Yeaah! Yeaaah! Have a taste of your own fucking medicine!"*

The Empress re-tightened her grip on Sam and drew him close to her roiling head. She opened a giant maw, revealing rows of glistening teeth like black bayonets and a throat to the depths of chaos.

Beatrice stared at the maelstrom. All of those souls, from an unguessable multitude of worlds. *Beneath flesh we are travelers in kind.* The implication in Cabal's words struck deep. Beatrice saw that Sam was losing. Garritch was on his hands and knees, gasping for breath. She recognized in herself a deep resistance, a potential to be more than she was bound by fear. The fear was in her mind. She looked down at her unshod feet, firm in contact with the macabre masonry, let go of resistance and yielded to change.

A force swept through her like a whirling wind. Her clothing deliquesced from her body and vanished. She became a truer version of herself, neither shamed nor impeded by nakedness. The faith that defined her core radiated outward and possessed her flesh.

Where her rosary had wrapped around her arm and melted into her skin, welts appeared. Fine links of silvery chain mail emerged through her skin and multiplied, enveloping her body up to her throat and encompassing all but her face. Where the crucifix had melted into her palm a cylindrical gold bar manifested and sprang into a formidable halberd. She felt a band embrace her head above her eyes.

Beatrice staggered under the transformation and sank to a knee. She touched the band on her brow. A diadem, it seemed, with a stone at its center. The time for doubt and confusion was done. She knew what she believed. It was required of her now to act, to adopt the precipitous mode of dispatch she so admired in Sam. She rose to her feet and breathed deep of the searing air.

She watched the thrashing, formless thing the Empress had become, seeking what she had sensed before, not self-deception but its root, the key organ of the being's consciousness, the kernel of hope denied at the heart of megalomania.

She couldn't see it. She thought of the blind artist and remembered how inner senses had guided her in the tunnel of mirrors. Another kind of vision was needed.

She closed her eyes. She could feel Garritch worn down to incapacity. She could feel Sam, his bright defiance, and, oh yes, she could feel the abomination that held him.

Beatrice saw it, the tiny spark of the thing that kept the monster alive, compressed almost to a singularity. Beatrice lowered her halberd, stepped, loped, charged and thrust her halberd deep into the monstrosity, impaling the spurned kernel of grace at its core.

With a shriek that cracked the walls and ceiling, the Empress loosened her grip on Sam. She pulled free of Beatrice's halberd and stared at her with a mass of astonished eyes. She groped for Beatrice, but her limbs lost integrity. Screaming in agony and frustration she began to shrink. Her form drew together into a knot that levitated briefly before dropping to the floor of the temple, where it liquified into a black pool.

Beatrice's halberd and chain mail withdrew into her flesh. She ran to Sam, who was slumped over like Garritch, rubbing his neck.

"Did we get her?" he gasped.

"She is gone."

"Well, sweet holy Christ, thank God."

Garritch stood, still breathing hard. He steadied himself, strode to the black pool and collected some of it in a glass vial, which he secured in an inner pocket of his long coat. He stared at Sam and Beatrice as if he hardly recognized them, then nodded and vanished.

"Where the hell did he go?"

"He quickened somewhere."

The walls were breaking apart, bones spitting across the floor. A large chunk of stone dropped from the ceiling.

"We'd better do that too, hadn't we?"

"To Lark's gate?"

Sam looked back. The force containing the maelstrom was destabilizing. The barrier was no longer uniformly flat but rippled and bulged.

"Try it."

Beatrice made the sign of the cross and closed her eyes. She opened them.

"No good?"

She shook her head fearfully. Sam pulled her close and wished them to Lark's celestial meadow. Nothing. A couple of columns shed stone and more chunks fell from the ceiling. Black fluid began to leak from the bone walls and rise from the seams between the floor stones around the Empress' remains.

Sam remembered something. "Come on, we got to get out of here. Do *not* step in that stuff."

They hurried through the temple, columns and walls collapsing about them. The maelstrom ate its way forward behind them, like a living mass of writhing gray sludge.

They dodged a fall of stone, made it to the door by the goddess statue.

Sam led Beatrice down the curved staircase. He glanced back at her. "What happened to your clothes?"

"I don't know!"

He threw his coat around her. "Come on."

A section of the stairway collapsed ahead of them. Sam hurried Beatrice toward the gap. "We're going to jump!"

"Okay!"

Beatrice landed on her feet, but Sam slammed into the far edge in the same damn place in his chest he had the bridge in Minuslitore. Beatrice caught his hand and helped him climb up.

"Go!" he shouted.

They ran to the bottom of the stairs. The domed ceiling breached, and the maelstrom ate through, sending down tendrils like searching tornadoes.

Sam pulled Beatrice left through the archway. The coffin was still there, leaning against the wall. He threw open the lid. The inside was bottomless, opening to a view of a meadow.

"In you go." Sam helped Beatrice into the coffin and she vanished. He followed her just as the walls collapsed around him.

Chapter Twenty-two

Four days out from Minuslitore, en route aboard the *Passenger* to new sights and deeper seas, Sam and Beatrice lay snuggled together in bed, facing the window, watching water go by.

"I keep thinking about those souls," Beatrice said.

Sam closed his eyes and listened to her breathe, grateful for every moment with her.

"If there is one covenant that should be inviolate between God and creation, it is the sanctity of a soul."

"Maybe they'll sort themselves out, now that she's gone."

"Do you think they will?"

"I do."

They were silent awhile.

"Do you think about Cabal?" Beatrice asked.

"Every day."

"I pray for him."

"So do I."

Beatrice sat up against the pillows. "Do you want children, Sam?"

Sam squirmed up and lay his head on her chest. "Sure, let's have lots." He sensed he'd misunderstood, looked up at her. "Or not."

"It wouldn't matter to you?"

He sat up beside her. "Well, I guess I feel like I've got so much now, anything more would be gravy."

She looked out at the water.

"What's going on?"

She let out a long sigh. "Every day, when I wake up … I do not know how to tell you this."

"Just tell me."

"I'm renewed."

He frowned. "What do you mean?"

"I'm back to the way I was before. As if we'd never … done anything."

He stared. His eyes widened with understanding.

"I think it has something to do with the archetype I've become."

"Are you sure? How do you know?"

"I know."

He took a moment to digest the information. "So, am I … am I *hurting* you, every time?"

Beatrice loved the concern in his eyes but couldn't help laughing. She took hold of his hand. "Not so much that I want you to stop."

She rested her head on his shoulder and he put his arm around her. "Lady, you are something else."

"I love making love with you, Sam. You're a wonderful lover."

He scratched his chin, mugging skepticism. "You don't have anyone to compare me to."

"That's true." Beatrice furrowed her brow at him, pretending to consider it. "I should try it out with other men. Women too, maybe. I think Sheply's taken an interest."

Sam cleared his throat in disapproval.

"But you make a fair point. I don't have much experience with sex. Far less than you, I'm sure."

"Not so much as you might think. You *are* the same person who was a nun when we met, or what have you done with her?"

"I've changed."

"I'll say."

"I might change more."

"Really. Care to expand on that?"

"Well, down here, as far as I can tell, anything goes. I might become the Exalted Mistress of Mutual Mass Orgasm, or some such."

"Is that right."

"Anything's possible."

"Well, His High Lord of That's-Not-Funny wishes to inform Her Illustrious Ladyship that, in spite of the supernatural cool he's thus far exhibited escorting her around buck naked in front of all and sundry, he is fully capable of turning bat shit Neanderthal should anyone make a serious play to horn in on his action."

"Her Highness is pleased to hear it. In a very uncharacteristic, un-nun-like way."

Sam pulled her close. "You're the Queen of my heart, lady."

She drew him into her arms, and they made an ocean of their own.

Hours later, Gan knocked on the door. Virgin slid under the covers. Sam pulled on his pants and let him in.

"Two points of order," Gan announced.

"Proceed, Captain," Sam said.

"Point one: The crew and I are agreed that persons who save the universe should travel for free. You are therefore welcome to sail with us for as long and whenever you like, fare and expenses waived."

"Thank you, Gan," Beatrice said. "That's very kind and generous. Please extend our gratitude to the crew."

"Yeah, thanks, brother," Sam said.

"Point two," he spoke to Beatrice, "I have instructed the crew that they are not to stare at you when you go on deck. Anyone caught ogling will be summarily keelhauled."

Beatrice frowned. "That's a bit extreme. They can hardly be blamed for looking."

"My ship, my rules."

"Do these rules extend to you?"

"Of course not. I'm the captain."

Beatrice laughed.

"The point," Gan said with seriousness, "is that you should feel at liberty to go about the ship, confident that you will be accorded every respect."

"Thanks, Cap'n."

"Yes, thank you, Gan."

Gan bowed. "Supper in one hour."

Beatrice looked out the window at the jungle going by on a wild coastline. "That's it," she murmured.

"What?"

"My name. It's what the Labyrinth insists that I be." She gave Sam a bemused look. "Virgin."

Sam didn't like it, but he knew she was right, the moment the word left her lips. He started to object but shook his head resignedly. "All right, sister, Virgin it is."

They went up to Gan's cabin. The senior crew members wished them a hearty welcome. The table was laid with baked fish, stewed vegetables, bread, cheese, fruit and pitchers of ale. Gan gestured for them to take seats on either side of him at the head of the table. Virgin sat down across from the man she loved, comfortable in her own skin, in full possession and authority of her person.

Epilogue

Cabal fell through the maelstrom of desperate disintegrating souls. He was concerned about what would become of them. Perhaps, in the fullness of time, they would exhaust their panic and piece themselves back together, though that seemed unlikely.

They were dangerous. Even without the Empress to guide them, they might graze other worlds and Labyrinths and do great harm. They needed in their midst an ameliorating presence—a guide. He considered if and how he might fulfill that need, though it was not a task he desired.

All of the ways he thought of were almost certain to fail. He wanted to leave. It would be difficult enough to free himself and return to Earth. If he could, indeed, do that.

He could do a great many things that no one else could—no one he had ever met. The universe, with its many planes, was a very big place. Undoubtedly there were manifold beings with capacities as great or greater than his own. None of them, at present, nearby.

This should be a job for God. A mess like this having been made, God should clean it up.

Cabal believed in God, a benevolent God, though he never discussed the matter. He did not care if anyone shared his belief or agreed with it. The problem with beliefs, though, was that one could never be entirely certain that they were true. If he abandoned the maelstrom, he would never be free of wondering what became of it.

He thought of one thing he could do. It would cost him dearly, and he would be forever changed, to an extent he could neither control nor predict.

It had been a long while since Cabal had smiled. He had dealt with a great many devious and malicious persons in his long existence, and a large measure of them had been accomplished smilers. So Cabal had given it up. He'd given up frowning for the same reason.

It occurred to him that his presence in this place, at a time when help was needed that only one such as he or God might provide, could be interpreted as an indication that his belief was tenable. The thought amused him, and just that once he permitted himself to smile.

After all, no one was watching.

About the Author

Stephen T. Vessels is a member of the Pre-Joycean Fellowship and a Thriller Award nominated author whose stories have appeared in Ellery Queen Mystery Magazine, The Santa Barbara Literary Journal, releases from ShadowSpinners Press, Grey Matter Press and other publications. Of his story collection *The Mountain & the Vortex and Other Tales*, reviewer Chris Wozney wrote, "Vessels seems to have distilled the essence of Harlan Ellison, Lovecraft, Zelazny … and certainly something of himself, to produce a brandy the gods would savor."

Stephen is also a visual artist. Currently he works predominantly in ink, using the same pen he writes with. A one-man show of his work exhibited three years ago at the Andre Zarre Gallery in New York City. Stephen writes and draws every day.

The Ruptured Firmament is Stephen's second published novel. Among his many ongoing projects he is writing a third book for the Labyrinth of Souls series.

Stephen's favorite piece of classical music is Ferruccio Busoni's Piano Concerto in C Major. He recommends Marc Andre Hamelin's performance, which can be heard on YouTube.

stephenvessels.com

The Original
DUNGEON SOLITAIRE
Tomb of Four Kings

Still Available for Free
at

matthewlowes.com/games

Complete Rules
are Print-Ready and Playable
with any Standard Deck
of Playing Cards

Dungeon Solitaire
Labyrinth of Souls

Complete Rulebook
&
Labyrinth of Souls Tarot Deck
Available at
matthewlowes.com/games

Labyrinth of Souls Fiction
Eleven books available now!

coming soon
Aftermath by Cynthia Coate-Ray

For more information, visit
shadowspinnerspress.com